on the count of
THREE

AJ NICOLE

Copyright © November 2023 by AJ Nicole.

2nd Edition

All rights reserved. Books By AJ Nicole.

No portion of this book may be reproduced in any form without written permission from the publisher or author, except as permitted by U.S. copyright law, except for use of brief quotations in book reviews, etc.

This is a work of fiction. Including but not limited to all names, characters, places, and events are either the products of the author's imagination or used in a fictitious manner. Any resemblance to actual people, living or dead, is purely coincidental and not intended by the author.

All brand names and product names used in this book are trademarks, registered trademarks, or trade names of their respective holders. AJ Nicole is not associated with any product or vendor used in this book and does not own the rights to products or vendors used in this book.

Published by AJ Nicole, Books By AJ Nicole

Cover Designed by Books By AJ Nicole

Proofread/Edited by AJ Nicole and Maryann Syler

AUTHOR'S NOTE

This story is hot.
Like, you might get burned.
Or maybe you're used to the heat.
Perhaps it's not hot enough?
Regardless, this book has breeding kink, daddy kink, some force and a sprinkle of rough stuff.
There's three of them and one of her.
Stalker vibes.
Two at once.
Delicious wrestlers who dirty talk.
It's not meant to be deep or swoon worthy. It's meant to be fast, hot, fun, and done.
So love it or hate it, but I hope you'll enjoy the ride.

For the fantasies that hide in the dark.

How dare you?

Zipper – Jason Derulo
All That Glitters – Earl
Reverse – Sage The Gemini
Such a Whore – JVLA (stellular remix)
Confident – Demi Lovato
Fuck Away the Pain – Divide The Day
Lights Down Low – Maejor, Waka Flocka Flame
Lolly – Maejor, Juicy J, Justin Bieber
Bad Bitch – Bebe Rexha, Ty Dollar Sign
Mount Everest - Labrinth

One
Nova

Honestly, I didn't expect to be here. The bright white lights scatter across the ceiling, shining harshly, but charmingly down into the arena. The ring is illuminated like the star of the show, and rightfully so. I've only ever seen it a few times in person, but it's usually occupied with dirty men or rowdy women, and it's never looked so pristine and innocent before. Plus I was like a million years younger and now, I'm looking at it with new and more appreciative eyes.

Empty seats surround the stadium, the walkway is clear all the way up to the entrance stage. It's surreal. It's kind of like walking into a movie theater to watch something on the big screen and you get the entire theater to yourself. Or like running up to the ice cream truck on a Saturday afternoon, seven years old, in hopes for a Choco-Taco and there's only one left. It's all yours.

The feeling is incompatible to the reputation of bloodshed, danger, and power that is claimed here. Instead, it's a different kind of power I see when I glaze over this intensely beautiful place. A power that holds both truth and idea. The truth is, it's just a ring. A wood-planked stage layered with a foam mat surrounded by three natural fiber tape-wrapped ropes held together by turnbuckles, or the big leather balls as I used to call them. But that's the truth of the ring; in all of its glory, quiet and mysterious.

The idea, it's the center of destruction and peril and the very ground beneath some of the world's most creatively dangerous characters. Fake or not. And it's the home of entertainment enjoyed by millions around the world.

Standing in this empty arena feels like a rewrite of a previous dream. It feels like a bonus chapter to my story, knowing I was always meant to flip the page to this exact scene but it's all brand new.

I remember sitting ringside in this exact arena, back when I was just a little girl who wore pigtails and denim overalls. My braces took up most of my mouth and I probably had a unibrow. My mom would hold me on her lap as we watched my dad beat the shit out his opponents—or so I'd like to think. It was usually the other way around though.

Never the champion. Always the hero.

That's the way professional wrestling works. And despite popular belief, not all wrestling is scripted. Okay, ninety-nine-point-nine percent of it may be scripted *now*. But Daddy let me in on a little secret when he retired, most of the stuff we saw on T.V was in fact in real life and in real time.

But it's all a distant memory now, and I know that things have changed since then. The long road trips, the chaos of the violent art. Professional wrestling put a strain on my parents' relationship. And it also took a toll on me.

Even after he retired, even after the ring lights turned off and the arena went dark.

Despite the glory that my dad's career brought him, it brought sadness and neglect to me and my mom. Daddy's career was always more important than his family it seemed, though he tried to play it off like he was a big family man when the cameras were rolling.

I just know he'd pay more attention to me if I were born a boy like he wanted. He wanted a legacy to follow in his footsteps, to wrestle like he did. And I didn't really want to do that.

Girls can wrestle too, in fact it's much bigger for us females now than it used to be, but I just didn't want to live my life neglecting my family like my dad did to us.

I wish I could tell my dad how he made me feel, how *little* I was to him. But after he went out with my mom for some errands, leaving me with the neighbor, I never saw them again.

He wrapped his car around a tree taking my mom's life with him.

Some say he was drunk and it was an accident. Others say he did it on purpose because he had mental issues and wrestling can cause some major trauma to the head. I like to believe that my parents were enjoying a nice ride to wherever they were going and a sweet, helpless little deer jumped out in front of them, causing my dad to swerve off the road and the entire thing was just a big freak accident.

I was nine when that happened. My dad had just retired a few months before and I'll never learn what caused the accident. Because I refused to look into it or listen to what reports said had happened.

I believe in my own story for the sake of my heart and I'm okay with knowing that I might be lying to myself.

I'm okay pretending that my dad loved me when he died. But I hate that he took a piece of my self-worth with him.

"Nova Satterlee?" A male voice sounds from behind me, echoing around the arena, making his way from the stairs in the stands and down to center stage where I still stand in utter disbelief.

"That's me." I turn to see Shawn McMillin. The owner of it all.

I remember watching him on screen as well. Him and his dad, Victor, have a very large reputation in the wrestling world—or more so their ego is very large which takes up half the space of this arena, almost like a fog lingering thickly above us as the clicks of his probably-too-expensive dress shoes gets closer to where I'm standing. However, together, Victor and Shawn McMillin maintained one of the greatest sports ever to be aired on television, if you ask me, and to this day the business alone is bringing in billions. And despite the utter stench of arrogance that permeates off of Shawn–I can smell it the closer he gets–this world of wrestling has kept the interest of thousands and thousands of people by stabilizing entertainment in their homes all because of a dream that the McMillin family had.

Which is similar to why I'm here. *A dream.*

One I might not be able to understand but I followed my heart and this is where it led me.

He finally approaches me with his navy-blue suit, slicked back, graying hair, black loafers—they are in fact too expensive—and a very cocky smile. He's got the kind of on-screen personality that people despise because, naturally, he did that himself for the entertainment of millions all to secure the views. I'm just hoping his hubristic attitude and grossly alarming entitlement is *only* for the camera.

"Welcome to UWE." Shawn's hands go wide as he gestures to the world in front of us. UWE stands for United Wrestling Entertainment, and it's the biggest and *baddest* in the world.

"So glad to finally meet you. My assistant told me great things about you, including your passion for the sport." He tips his head up toward the ring, expecting me to follow his eyesight and completely underestimating the fact that women have a sixth sense for *pervy-ism* which is what hints me to his disgusting attempt to sneak a glance at my chest when he thinks I've looked away.

Barf.

I knew I should have dressed more conservatively, mentally cursing myself for thinking sexy was more important than respect in a moment of desperation to want to fit in. I know this scene and I know it's an environment filled with men but this dress called to me when I went through my closet and I've always enjoyed wearing things that accentuated the curvature of my body because I've never been stick-skinny. My dress is a long-sleeve, black blazer-dress with a deep neckline and gold button accents that are actually functioning buttons seeing as they're what's holding my dress together. It hits about a few inches above my knees so it's not too short but with the added appeal of my thick, tan legs–thanks to my velvet-black pumps–I look a little taller which makes my dress look a little shorter.

Before I can allow myself to feel any more nerves, I shake off the invasion of Shawns eyes and I smile at him like I know how. Sweet but professional. Then, I take a deep breath and nod my head.

"Yes, I'm very excited to start. I remember watching my dad right here-"

"Right, so we really should get you to the meeting," he interrupts me, and I almost have to force myself to not blink aggressively, which is something I would do if trying to attentively look for the audacity of this mother fucker if only to shove it down his throat.

But he's my boss now. So, I swallow down the sudden urge to call this man a raging dick for being so disrespectful and let him get away with it…this time.

I don't usually let people step all over me so easily. I've had to make my own way in this world after my parents' death and I damn well know that women hardly stand a chance as it is. But in a world as cutthroat as this, sometimes you have to pick and choose the battles worth fighting for and having this ignorant slug of a man interrupt me isn't something I'm going to let fester.

"Of course," I respond, not wanting to say anything he'd feel obligated to interrupt.

"Right this way."

I have no idea what to expect, but it's my time to shine.

Shawn leads me up the walkway through the entrance behind the stage. I only ever imagined what it would be like to walk down this runway with a big entrance, fancy fire shows, loud music, and all of the confidence in the world.

I've seen so many do it when I'd watch the shows, either from the front row of the stadium or from the plush carpet of my home.

My dad's walk-down song was some kind of over-the-top rendition of *Sabotage* by the Beastie Boys and he always had the craziest lights thrown around the stadium.

We turn a corner down to another hall and I let out a sigh of anticipation when we stop at a red door and he reaches to turn the knob.

Shawn opens the door to a large, dimly lit conference room. I'm not prepared for him to put his hand on my lower back to scooch me through the threshold of the doorframe, feeling myself inwardly cringe.

"Would you like to introduce yourself?" Shawn is so close to me—too close.

Though he's not too much taller than my five-four, it just feels like he's overcrowding me in every way possible, and it doesn't help that he smells like fried onions despite how nicely he's dressed.

"Hi, I'm Nova Satterlee. I'm joining the creative writing team as a writer's assistant." I nod my head, smiling confidently as I make eye contact with as many people as I can in the room.

I impress myself with my ability to speak, but really, I've never been one with stage fright. I've always done pretty well in large crowds and group tasks. I almost always end up taking the lead while others slide by like floaters, allowing me to take full reign on whatever it was we'd be working on.

Watching my dad maneuver a crowd the way he did really gave me inspiration to be just as big and bold as him one day. Though I'm more reserved about my confidence whereas wrestlers show it off like a fancy car.

I also knew that I needed to make sure that I presented myself in a respectable way before others automatically shunned me to the confined shadows of my dad's failure as an on-screen hero. Because people *have* actually done that before, called me the product of a loser.

I really did get made fun of for who my dad was despite being a big star. Sure, he lost a few times—okay, a lot of times—but he did it with pride and honor and he never let his character become something he wasn't. *Evil.*

But I laugh at the irony knowing damn well that my dad was kind of a dick in real life. Especially when it came to the likes of his own daughter.

So, even though I'm nervous and anxious for this to go the way I want it, I take after my dad and conjure up all of my confidence, never letting it waver no matter what people might think of me. Until…

Dark.

Black.

Irises.

My breath hitches as I feel the power radiating from the stare of a pair of dark, black irises. I can feel the fight for attention in them as they burn through my skin. First up, then down. *Did I just get chills?*

I look away for a brief second, the control I had just seconds ago disappearing as I attempt to swallow the lump in my throat. I tuck my hair behind my ear, trying to pretend to focus on what Shawn has started rambling about. But even my ears aren't paying attention. Every nerve ending in my body is buzzing with the need to look back up, to see those eyes which I can feel burning into my skin.

But I force myself to keep my head down for a few moments longer, needing to suppress the violent heat that's spreading over the surface of my skin in a wave of goosebumps.

Just when I finally think I've gained some kind of control over my suddenly debilitated self, I look over to Shawn first to see him throwing his hands around in some kind of frantic manner, really diving in deep about shit that has nothing to do with me or much more this company, really.

And then I feel it again.

The gravitational pull of a heated gaze, begging me to look its way.

But this time when I look up, I feel the melting sensation of ice swarm my skin as he smirks at me and it creates a feeling so feral in me, I almost don't know what to do next, breathing included. I'm so taken aback by the sudden rush of liquid heat pooling between my thighs, I have to force my eyes to break from his soul-searing gaze. But I only get so far before I find myself curiously wondering over the rest of him.

His golden-brown skin is marked with some tribal tattoos, covering the entirety of his right arm from his shoulder down to his wrist. Long, thick, curly black hair is tied up into a top-knot revealing a shaved undercut. A strong jawline that tenses as he grinds his teeth. Those dangerously dark eyes are still raking up and down my body in a fit of what looks severely too close to hunger.

Of course, *I know who this is.*

This is one of the most villainously characterized men in the business right now. He's all bark and even more bite. And I've been watching him for years.

Zayden Stone.

He is just as beautiful in person as he is on the screen. Even more so, really. The features of this man paint so many incredibly forbidden fantasies in my head. Fantasies I know are too far out of the realm for discussion.

He's too close, even though he sits the furthest back in the room. The room is just not big enough to hold the tension currently gripping me as he stares at me, and I squirm under the involuntary attack of pebbles taking wave over my body.

I have to remain professional if they're ever going to respect me, especially once they find out who my dad is; *the guy who always lost.* But it's silly of me to assume they don't already know.

Does he really have to keep staring at me like that?

I blush recalling the time he ripped his shirt in two as he prepared to battle his opponent, revealing the scripted sentence that follows down his back against his spine. Though, I've never been close enough to read what it says.

My body heats thinking maybe now I'll finally get the chance.

In a sudden moment, I'm shaken out of my trance when I feel the slimeball next to me place his hand on my shoulder, hearing that he's already talking about my father, which makes me wince a little.

But I can't expect anyone here to not bring up my father—he played a big role in his day—so I push down the overwhelming feeling of abandonment and put on my best Satterlee smile as Shawn continues to talk wrestling politics like the showman that he is, and I look around the room once more only to be caught off guard by a piercing blue light.

But it's not a light at all really, it's more of a reflective, metaphorical light coming from another set of eyes. Of course, everyone is looking in my direction, and though I didn't anticipate being gawked at by Zayden Stone, I also don't expect to be captivated by eyes that are less familiar to me.

Hunter Dodge.

He's the bad boy with the school-boy smile. His short, blonde hair hangs in wet, tight curls just over his ocean-colored eyes, which eat me up just as Zayd's did seconds ago. Hunter has a blank canvas of pale skin, shirtless so that I can see every hard inch of his body. Heat radiates over my skin as I try not to play victim to his stare. But it's all too much.

He's newer to the lineup of UWE. But he's climbed his way to the top of the bad boy's club rather quickly, mainly because he's a hit with the ladies which means he makes for a great storyline addition.

I see him whisper something under his breath and I shift my gaze slightly to look at the person sitting next to him, and it's apparent they're both talking about me. I can't seem to escape the attack of butterflies as I watch honey brown eyes *also* tearing through my soul like a category five tornado.

Krew Rivers.

His complexion is tanned next to Hunter's and is home to minimal black tattoos in the form of scripted words and various flowers and roman numerals. His deep brown hair is styled in a disconnected undercut giving him a deadly but dapper appeal. The thick of his facial hair is trimmed perfectly while still looking gruff and he's etched like a fucking god.

They all are.

I break his stare to look at the room as a whole and everyone else is now watching Shawn, but these three men stay staring at me.

I lose my focus, everything feeling too hot and too overwhelming. I'm here to do a job, my dream job, not be gawked at by barbaric men who bleed and bruise for a living.

Everything I thought about being here, living out my dream, following lightly in my father's footsteps, feeling a sense of power, was all wrong.

I wasn't supposed to feel like this.

Claimed.

I try to pull my focus back onto Shawn, who is now rambling about his father's legacy and some bullshit about honor and pride, none of which he possesses himself.

But I feel the pull of the hardened stares again and of course, curiosity gets the best of me. Do they know that they're staring at me? Do they even recognize each other, all three of them ripping me in half with just their eyes? Those dangerous, mesmerizing, god-fearing eyes. And why do I suddenly feel warm all over?

It's at this very moment, I know that there's no way I'll be able to work with these men willingly. With, near, or around. Good thing they're the main-screen personalities and I'm just a background character because the tension is too much.

They're quite the opposite of everything I believe in. Dark, rude, monstrous. They're the villains of the stories that play out on Monday and Friday nights.

Always the champions. Never the heroes.

And I think I've just been sought out as their prize

Two

NOVA

After that horrifying meet and greet, Shawn let me know that the goal of the day is to get familiar with some of the wrestlers' schedules and the lay of the land. This is going to help me assist the creative writers as they prepare for the next big show in two days, which is Friday Night Beatdown. He gave me his assistant's phone number and told me to meet up with her for further details.

I know my dad would be proud of me, or at least that's what I tell myself because I don't really know what he'd think. I know he would have loved it if I would have wrestled instead, but watching female wrestlers growing up solidified the fact that I knew I didn't have a passion for it on a performance level.

I knew I always had more of an interest in the story being told. My imagination is what drew me toward wrestling to begin with.

Female wrestlers hold a bold stature and claim loud personalities that would severely overshadow the likes of my quiet confidence. I was never told I'd be good enough to perform on those levels so I just never imagined I could be like them. Maybe if I did get to spend more time with my father and learn some of the things he did, I might have gone that route instead. But writing is the career I opted for and the wrestling world has been a big part of my life, so here I am.

As I make my way to the top of the stairs and to the revolving door, a flash of bright white light blinds my vision along with the sound of a camera snapping a photo when I realize I've been captured by a nearby news reporter, or paparazzi, or whoever. I know they hang around here sometimes but why they'd want a picture of me strikes me as confused for a moment.

Unless.

They recognized who I am.

Nova Satterlee.

Daughter of David Satterlee.

Or to the rest of the world known as TKS—The Kind Soldier.

I know, it's cheesy. But it did fit his character pretty well to be honest. And obviously a little too much. And despite his burly, muscular build—almost like that of Hulk Hogan—he was truly a kind soldier on stage. He fought till the lights went out. And unfortunately, it didn't do him any good.

"Hurry up. Those idiots are like vultures for any kind of media they can get their hands on." A hand reaches down to the small of my back, startling me more than the flash of the camera did in the first place.

I look over to the source of the silky, soft timbre voice and see blonde hair and ice-blue eyes smiling at me with the most seductive school-boy smirk I've ever encountered.

But I don't let myself get lost for too long, stumbling inside as Hunter follows behind me.

"Thank you," I say as I struggle with my purse and phone.

"No problem, Nova." His tone is laced with cockiness as he says this to me. And I can't help but feel a small swarm of butterflies in my stomach. It's faint, but it's there, nonetheless.

"Word of advice. Don't eat your lunch outside. Camera creatures are everywhere." I smile at his creative term for the paparazzi and his gaze catches mine for a brief second in what seems like a flirtatious staring contest. But I shake my head subtly to break the stare and he moves his hand; my skin immediately misses the heat of his touch.

"Care to show me to the writing room?" I ask.

I spent the entire morning after the meeting sitting with Shawn's assistant who was supposed to be going over my list of things to do today. She didn't help much though, claiming Shawn didn't give her the best instructions on what to show me, so we spent all of two hours going over policy which I'd already done at home after I received the job offer. So basically, Caroline gave me the impression that she's assisting Shawn in more unconventional ways because I could tell she had no clue what she was doing.

By the time I decided to take my lunch break, I'd learned nothing.

"Right this way." He holds his hand out toward the lobby signaling me off to the right.

We walk down the long hallway—for what seems like more than a couple of minutes—passing doors on either side of us before eventually hitting the end corner of the building and turning right. Floor-to-ceiling windows give us a beautiful view to the landscaping outside on the right of us, while the other side houses old, framed photographs and trophies and news articles cased in glass and illuminated with recessed lighting.

I don't really notice when my feet come to a slow stop as I stare at some of the memorabilia. But then I see a news article from 1998, I was only about three years old at the time, and it's a headline of my dad's debut. Next to the article is a replica of a championship belt with his name etched in the gold center and the title of `heavy weight champion` just underneath.

"Your dad wasn't always a loser, little one." Hunter's soft tone creeps up behind me, I almost forgot he was here as I question how he answered the question I was forming in my head. But I don't turn away from the article when I answer him.

"I used to get bullied because he lost every single match," I admit. The feeling sits heavy in my stomach as a tear starts to form in my eye. Hunter lays a hand gently on my shoulder as I stare at everything in shock, disbelief, and *anger*.

He wasn't always a loser, but why did everyone seem to only bring up his losing streak? Why did I get picked on because of him, when he didn't even pay attention to me?

All of the negative thoughts flood me. Seeing this should bring joy to my heart, give me a sense of hope. Maybe it should give him a redeeming quality. But as I look at this photo of him—he's standing in the middle of the ring with the championship belt high in his hands—I see love in his eyes. Love for the moment, for his career, pure and utter love. It's probably what drove him to continue his faith in the company going forward.

But I've never seen him look at *me* like that.

He might have won this one match, maybe he even won more. But for most of his career he continued to accept defeat, even if it was scripted, and he continued to choose his career over his family over and over again. Meanwhile, his only child had to endure the wrath of cyber bullies and fans who were haters of TKS, even after his death. Dealing with the aftermath of someone she looked up to, someone she believed in even though she never saw this look of love in his eyes for *her*.

It's in that moment that I see my father in a different light. I now realize that I have been seeking out his approval because he never showed me I mattered to him and I was already a disappointment from the day I was born. So maybe I'm here for all the wrong reasons. Maybe this isn't my dream but just a way for me to continue to seek his acceptance even though he never really cared in the first place.

I feel Hunter squeeze my shoulder in what is meant to be an understanding and comforting gesture but it brings me out of thoughts.

I swipe the tear carefully away, not wanting to smear my mascara, before turning back down the hallway.

"We've been walking for several minutes, Mr. Dodge. Are we anywhere near the writing room?" I shake myself from the thoughts and decide to change the subject.

I take the only turn ahead of us, heading left around the hallway leading us to a set of double doors that open up to a part of the back area of the arena. Similar to the hallways that Shawn walked me through yesterday to get to one of the other meeting rooms.

"What is it that you're doing here again?" His tone is quieter in the hallways, an attempt to avoid echoes bouncing off the walls, though it's all steel and concrete back here.

"If you were paying attention at all yesterday, you'd know that I'm here as a writer's assistant," I snark back.

"I was paying attention yesterday. Trust me, little one." I stop and turn to look at him, but he keeps walking a few steps ahead before turning around. "Did you have to go to school for that?" he asks and I almost jerk my head in confusion, because why would he care? It's been a while since anyone has asked me anything remotely close to personal.

"Yeah, I took a ton of creative writing classes. I also have my degree in language arts and I also did some freelance writing throughout college." That's the gist of it. Nothing special really.

"I guess I never really paid attention to the parts that other people play here." He shoves his hands in his pockets, his arms flex as he does so, and I have to force my eyes shut and swallow to avoid the flush of red creeping up my neck. Because he is so fucking hot.

"Well, you also haven't been here long so I can see how the people who play the biggest part in what you do here can be swept under the rug. It's called *ignorance*, Mr. Dodge." I finally decide to respond as I look around and see absolutely no sign of a writing room.

I notice that he takes a curious few steps closer to me, but I pretend not to notice as I pull my phone from my purse. It's now two in the afternoon and I've wasted my entire day doing absolutely nothing productive from the mess with Caroline to this now stress-provoking encounter with Hunter.

Suddenly, I feel claustrophobic, like my air circulation is being cut short when I see how close Hunter is to me right now.

"Well, I'd say I'm definitely paying attention now, Miss Satterlee."

Three

NOVA

I feel the way my body reacts to his proximity. The adrenaline rush I get just from feeling him so close to me.

I *think* I don't want him this close, but there's betrayal in the way my skin prickles and the way my heart sounds in my ears.

This turns me on.

His calming and refreshing scent lingers in front of me, notes of saltwater mixed with a hint of amber dance beautifully across my nose.

"You are entirely, and inappropriately, too close to me right now, Mr. Dodge." I step back as he comes closer.

I force myself to require space though I know I *really* don't mind the intrusion. But before I know it, my back is up against the cold, hard concrete wall behind me, and he takes a few more steps to close me in.

His body is now crowding me, and everything feels like it's too much but not enough all at the same time. Like diving off a cliff into the crystal waters of the ocean, the sun beaming high in the sky and the seagulls creating sounds of lullaby as the cold saltwater splashes daringly against your skin. All to be swallowed whole by a great-white.

I watch the rise and fall of his chest as he drags his ocean eyes up my body in the most seductive, and enlivened way. But this is so fucking inappropriate.

"The way your heart is beating against your chest tells me that you kind of like it. Feel." Hunter grabs my suddenly sweaty hand from my side and peels my fingers from the fist I seemed to have formed, spreading them out before placing my palm over my chest.

He's right, it's beating hard and fast. Overwhelmingly so. Pounding in tandem with my uncontrollable breathing.

"You just caught me off guard is all." I force my hand out from under him which leaves his palm still placed on my chest. But instead of pushing him off or away like my clever brain is telling me to, I look at where the physical contact is, where his big hand is touching me. Because I am not as clever as the occupant rolling its eyes at me in my cranial cavity. And I feel something like liquid heat swirl between my thighs.

Hunter is dressed down in a pair of loosely hung jeans and a white t-shirt, which is more than he was wearing earlier. His skin is pale against my tan and his dirty-blonde hair—almost identical to my own—is flipped in a wavy mess.

This is so wrong. This is so incredibly wrong. To look at him with so much attraction lacing my eyes and damn well knowing that this is *not* normal.

"What about this, does this catch you off guard?" He removes his palm and uses his fingers to trace the outline of my dress. He starts from the collar near my neck and trails down to my cleavage over the curve of my breast until he reaches the first gold button. Using only one hand, the other bracing himself behind my head against the wall, he carefully fishes one of the buttons through its loop.

And I don't stop him.

My breath hitches when he gets it loose, then he moves to the next one. I feel my nipples harden painfully and I silently thank the dress for being a somewhat thicker material that he can't see through. But I catch his eye movement fluttering to that exact spot as he pulls another button loose, opening up my dress a little more.

I look down to see that he's unbuttoned enough buttons to see the top of my belly button, which wasn't hard considering the neckline was already deep to begin with. All he has to do is undo the last three buttons and he can slip my entire dress off my body.

Pebbles of pleasure scatter throughout the flesh of my breasts and I can feel our sensually-driven labored breaths intertwine.

His fingers are no longer trying to unbutton the rest of my dress however, which I'm not sure I'd even stop him.

"I'm actually not surprised that you're willing to force yourself on the first new girl you see, Mr. Dodge. So no, it doesn't catch me off guard that you're the type of *boy* who finds enjoyment in crowding a female with your overly confident ego more than it concerns me for our professional relationship together moving forward. Now, do you mind backing up so I can go find the human resources department?" I finally find the courage to push my palms against his chest, forcing him back an inch, but his rock-solid form is no match for me. Or maybe I didn't push hard enough, feeling the want that curls inside of me telling me that I'm weak to the man in front of me. Not strength wise, that's a given. But rather the other physical aspects. The one that sends signals of craving to the brain when in the presence of someone who looks the way Hunter does.

I'll be honest, my tone is stern and sure. Confident in my ability to make him think that I'm serious about putting a stop to the game he's playing. My biggest opposition, however, is the reaction of my body. I know he can tell that my actions speak louder than my words.

I start to button my dress back up, feeling him watch me intently as I do.

"You really want me to back up?" He leans in again but this time a little closer; I can feel his warm breath hit the surface of my cheek. "You sure you don't need my help? Because I can be an excellent helper." He takes this moment to place his hand just below the hem of my dress, slowly making his way under it.

Something feverishly erotic stirs deep in me. The threat of someone walking down the hallway to see us like this, and the filthy fact that I'm allowing this man to take advantage of me has me so fucking wet.

And even though I just pushed him off me, I don't stop him from playfully forcing himself on me again. Because it's not harmful and it doesn't hurt. It's gentle and intentional and I am actually drowning in how good it makes me feel. And maybe it's the fact I haven't been fucked in a very long time that prevents me from actually putting in any effort to pushing him off me a second time.

"But if you really want me to leave, little one, just say the word and I'll back off."

Lord, I don't know why but when he calls me *little one*, goosebumps are inevitable, and I know he can feel them as he trails his fingers higher up my thighs. He's so close to the curve of my ass.

"But I'd be lying if I said I wasn't physically drawn to you. And by the stutter in your breathing, I can tell you might feel the same. Or maybe it's been far too long for you and your body hasn't been used in a while. Used for all the great things a body like yours was made to do. So, tell me. Should I back up, Miss Satterlee?"

He's so close. So close I can feel his words plunging deep into the pool of pleasure inside me and swimming all the way down to where the ache throbs the most. So close I can feel . . . his erection. And I can't help but look, realizing there's still a few inches between us, *and I can feel his erection???*

I swallow an impossible lump of lust, feeling the urge to lick my lips, but I resist.

I have to stay strong and resist this man's charms. He's cocky and annoying, but so fucking charming.

Imagine that.

But before I find it in me to use my damned cowardly voice, another voice booms from behind Hunter, nearly making me jump under the perusal of his fingertips and eyes.

"Hunter. Get the fuck off her. McMillin needs us in his office." Hunter doesn't move, not a single skip of his flirtatious, overpowering beat.

I pull my dress down terrifyingly quickly. Hunter finally moves a little bit, only enough so that I can make out the face belonging to the thunderous voice.

Zayden.

He has a good six inches on Hunter. About ten inches on me. He's intimidatingly sexy. His dark features are even darker in the shadows of the hallway, only a few feet back. He's dressed in sweats and a t-shirt showing off only parts of the tattoo traveling up his arm. I don't look at him long, afraid of what my stupid body will do to betray me again.

Instead, I fold my arms at my chest and stare at Hunter like a kid who was told no at the toy store.

"I'll get off if she wants me to get off. Tell him, Nova. Do you want me to get off?" He still has one hand splayed against the wall behind me as he opens us up so that Zayd can see better.

I'm embarrassed. Ashamed.

But only because I enjoyed what was happening just now, not that we were nearly caught.

"I said get the fuck off." Zayd takes a step closer toward us, the dim lighting in the back hallways allows for the glimmer of his wet curls to shine in the midst of the shadows and I can see the demand in his eyes. It's terrifyingly gripping. And the tone of his voice sounds almost territorial.

"Jesus, Zayd. I was just showing Nova around." Hunter backs up entirely, holding his hands up in surrender and I feel as though a boulder has been lifted off my chest. But I grow to miss the warmth.

That's when I accidentally catch another glimpse of Zayd, and this time he isn't staring at me, he's staring *through* me. Like *I'm* the one who was in the wrong here. Like he's pissed at *me* for the actions of his colleague.

My whole body feels like it's burning with the heat of his harsh glare.

"McMillin's. Now." Then he storms off.

I'm still leaning against the wall when I consider the fact that Hunter will go back to his teasing touches and whether I'd let him proceed again or not. I'm so fucking hot. And I don't know what's gotten into me. Even when I take time to get to know a boy or show my interest in someone, I'd never let them touch me as quickly as I surrendered to Hunter's curiously dirty mind just now.

Hunter takes a few steps back, his eyes not leaving my body until he turns away, leaving me ashamed and frustrated. Flushed and humiliated.

"Turns out the writer's room is on the other side of the building, just thought I'd take you on a little detour. I'll see you around, little one."

Jesus, I'm so incredibly fucked. And stupid.

"Asshole," I yell after him as he walks away and chuckles.

Incredibly fucking stupid

WRESTLING

LITTLE STAR

little one

Four

Nova

Once I'd finally made it over to the writer's room, I was exhausted. My feet were hurting and my pride was shot.

The writing team, though all men, were pretty decent to follow along with and did an upstanding job going over the ins and the outs of what they do. Not that all men are incompetent, I just mean that they didn't ogle me the whole time. Well most of them didn't. They even said that though I'm just the assistant, there's a chance that my ideas could be used for any of the upcoming shows. Though I do miss the presence of the one person I was looking forward to meeting, the head creative writer. I wonder when I'll get to meet him.

The other writers told me that they sometimes write all the way up to the minutes before the live show starts, even if the idea isn't complete. So having me around might make it a bit easier to save some time.

We went over some of the anticipated match ups over the next few weeks and they talked about the creative writing behind this week's story.

It's no surprise to find out that one of the main events for Friday is a tag-team match featuring Hunter and Krew and their opponents, the UKO brothers—the Ultimate Knock Out brothers. They've been in an ongoing feud for months now and each match is another match closer to the championship match. We all know it's *the* match to determine who the new owners of the championship belts will be. Right now, Hunter and Krew hold the title of tag-team champions.

The most anticipated match though features Zayden Stone. He's slated to go against his arch nemesis, Gryffin, The Irish Hero. He's well known for his Irish accent and bright red hair. He's handsome and seems genuine enough on television, but as usual, the heroes always lose. Their rivalry is one that goes back a few years and has just gotten bigger and bigger over time.

After gathering all the vital information I need for the next few weeks, I head toward the cafeteria to go over some of my notes and jot some other things down. I order an iced coffee from the coffee cart and find a seat somewhere I can take my shoes off and no one will see. Which isn't hard considering there's hardly anyone here.

"Mind if I sit?" A familiar voice creeps up from behind me and I don't have to look to know who it is.

I roll my eyes as he sits next to me, throwing one leg over each side of the bench and I cringe thinking he'll see my bare feet under the table.

"Do you ever go away, Mr. Dodge?"

"I need to eat too. Not my fault the only place to do that is in the cafeteria," he responds in a sarcastic tone.

I look over to see that he doesn't have a single item of food in his possession.

"So, were you gonna go get that food then or did you just want to sit here and annoy me?" I don't know what possesses me to talk to him like that, because the smirk that creeps across his face only proves that he likes it when I give an attitude.

"Already ate. Was just leaving when I saw you sit down."

"Lucky me," I quip.

He clicks his tongue.

"Besides, I thought maybe I'd try to pick up where we left off." His words would sound slimy coming from any other man, yet spilling from the tone of his voice, they don't sound so cringe.

But that doesn't stop me from taking the moment to call him out.

"You're a pig," I state, sliding my heels back on and picking up my shit, opting to move away since he won't.

"No, I'm *persistent*."

I don't stop at his words, despite how innocent they may sound. I know he's just trying to be flirty, but I can't enable his behavior. Especially considering what I let him get away with earlier.

"Wait." He gets up from his seat and jogs over to me.

"Hunter, I don't have time for whatever the hell you have planned." I turn on my heels to face him and I nearly knock into him as he stops in front of me, but before anything can fall from my hands he reaches out and stops everything from crashing to the ground.

"You're right, I'm a pig. I'm sorry." He looks at me with puppy eyes, eyes that are as blue as the deepest parts of the ocean. I can tell he's trying to be genuine, but it could also all be a ruse to get me in bed with him.

And honestly, as much as I respect myself and demand not to be treated like a fresh piece of ass, I probably would get into bed with him. If he were anyone else and we didn't work together. I probably would have let him fuck me up against the cold hallway wall earlier.

Because my sexual frustration has been a far-too long battle and a girl's vibrator can only do so much. I curse myself for feeling the way I do but try to feign being unbothered.

Though when I look at the way Hunter is looking at me, a fire ignites low in my belly. Because he's actually *looking* at me. My eyes, my chest, my stomach, my legs. And though the realization would normally make me feel uncomfortable, I actually feel really flattered under his gaze.

"I didn't mean to come off the way I did earlier. I guess I just got lost in your attraction and when you didn't push me away…" he trails off for a second before taking in a deep breath. "I'm sorry. I should have never put you in that position."

"Who *are* you?" I ask in a sarcastic tone.

Hunter is an egotistical wrestler. In fact, they all are. But I haven't heard much about him being romantically involved with anyone so the assumption is that he's a player and here I am feeding right into his game.

"I'm just a man, Nova. I wrestle and I might come off as cocky sometimes, but at the end of the day, I'm not blind to someone as pretty as you. And before you ask, I'm not a player. I can see what you're thinking." I roll my eyes when he says this. "I know I came off as one just now, but again, I couldn't ignore your attraction."

"You stating that you had to practically force yourself on me because I'm hot makes you sound *exactly* like a player, Mr. Dodge."

"You're right, it does. And I'm sorry." His phone starts to ring, and I feel uncomfortable standing here with all this shit in my hands.

"Just a second," he says to me before he turns around to answer his phone.

I take this moment to make my escape, turning as fast I can and walking—no, jogging—toward the exit.

But I don't make it far before I hear his footsteps catching up to me. He reaches for my elbow and when he makes contact, he spins me back around so that I'm facing him, flush with his chest. All of my stuff squished painfully between us.

He looks down at me with an intense, heated glare that bleeds the sarcasm of betrayal as he continues his phone conversation and he uses his thumb and index finger to lightly pinch my chin, forcing my gaze up to his.

"Yes, I got it. I'll be there." He ends the call and lets go of my chin at the same time, allowing a few inches of space to fall between us as I back up feeling so much contact, feigning appreciation for the space but damn well knowing my body craves to be touched.

"Why did you try to leave just now?" He sounds disappointed, but only enough for me to know that he's not really hurt, he just wanted me to stick around.

I opt not to answer. I can't. I feel stuck between the space of wanting him to put his hands on me again and wanting to stand my ground and not take whatever egotistical game he's playing.

"Fine. Don't answer me. But I really want to make it up to you. Ya know, for being all alpha-male on you earlier."

"And for taking me around the building earlier when I trusted you to take me where I needed to go," I add. "My feet will never recover," I quip. Not forgetting that this asshole also led me to the opposite side of the building just to fuck with me.

"That too. Again, I'm sorry. Listen, there's a party tonight. At the Punch Bowl Social. It's downtown. If you want to get out tonight, maybe hang out with me and I can buy you a drink to make up for being a douche, I'll be there around nine." He lets the invitation roll off his tongue in a sexy tone of genuine interest.

"That might be just as douchey as you throwing me up against the wall earlier," I say shifting the contents in my hands around.

"I'm sorry, Nova. I'm obviously not saying the right things here. But you can't blame me for wanting to hang out with the prettiest girl in town. I promise I don't mean to come off as a douche. It's just a casual party, nothing fancy. Just some of the wrestlers getting together and hanging out. And I promise I won't even breathe the same air as you without your permission." He looks down at me, and again gives me those fucking blue eyes.

Hunter is attractive, I can't deny it. And I can't fault him for earlier. He asked me several times if I wanted him to back off and I didn't tell him no. Because deep down I wanted him closer. But I also didn't want to submit to that feeling.

The idea that someone I've seen on T.V, someone as good-looking as Hunter, was standing in front of me and touching my body, is something I'd never imagined would really happen.

I think over his invitation, and I decide I really will consider it. It might be fun to go out for the night. I don't know anyone in the area since relocating so I might be able to make some friends. It also might give me some cred with the wrestlers and anyone else who might be there.

"Okay. *If* I go out tonight, I'll hold you to that douchey gesture of buying me a drink," I say while turning around to finally free myself of the overwhelmingly closeness in space we share.

"Anything you want, little one," he shouts behind me and it's the last two words that have me crumbling in the knees, knowing that no amount of self-respect in the world will hold up to him calling me that stupid nickname.

WRESTLING

LITTLE STAR

Five

Nova

I can't believe I'm doing this. I'm here, begrudgingly standing in this stupid line at this stupid club waiting to get in, all because I crave being seen by someone like hunter. *Pathetic.*

It's nearly ten at night now and I know there's a chance I've missed Hunter, but I decided that I wasn't coming for him. I decided to come and have a good time, maybe meet some new people and make some friends.

But now, I'm regretting it. Because even though I've changed my clothes from earlier–now sporting a tight leather skirt, an oversized *Metallica* tee tied at my belly button, and some white converse–my feet are still killing me. And standing in this line for about thirty minutes now hasn't helped.

The line moves up a little and a few more guys head in, flashing their ID's and handing over their cover to the bouncer. A few girls waltz up on the side of me and everyone else in line, wearing the flashiest dresses dripped in sequin and jewels with hair that blows mine out of the water might I add. They flash the bouncer their white smiles instead of their ID's, playing the flirty roles as they throw their hair behind their shoulders causing their chests to bounce a little and the bouncer lets them right in. I roll my eyes at the scene.

I hear my phone chime, just as I feel a couple of raindrops hit the top of my head. *Great.* Before reaching for my phone, I gather my hair and throw it into a high ponytail, not wanting the curls to ruin in the rain.

I look at my phone to see a text message from an unknown number that reads:

> Text me when you're here.

I can only assume that it's Hunter. But how he got my number is beyond me.

I decide to chance it, and text back.

> I've been here.

And within almost thirty seconds, I look up and see Hunter whispering in the bouncer's ear as he waves me over.

Everyone turns to glare at me, almost envious that I get to skip the line. And I hate the way that feels but also, I kind of enjoy it at the same time.

As I approach Hunter, I take in his outfit. God is he sexy as hell. He's wearing a pair of light wash jeans with destruction just above the knees and he's wearing a black barely-buttoned button up. His blonde hair is in a mess of wet looking waves that hang over his eyes. My mouth does this thing where it waters. *Strangest thing.*

Hunter leads me into the bustling club, palm on the small of the back and I duck my head to hide my smile because my body likes it too much when his hands are on me. I see purple and blue strobes bounce off the dark walls.

There are strippers in cages in every corner of the club, fully naked as they straddle poles and touch each other, and a DJ is upstairs blasting hip hop and techno beats as people dance too-closely to each other on the dance floor below. There's a bar placed in the back of the club that houses only the most expensive bottles of liquor and each wall surrounding it has a VIP room.

"Didn't think you were coming, little one." Hunter takes me to the VIP room to the left of us. It's all glass walls so you can still look out into the club itself and there's no door, just a rope that another bouncer is guarding.

Hunter gets us in and instantly I recognize a few of the occupants. I notice Krew, who seems to sense my presence as well because he eyes me down as a few handsy females sit around him. Or on him. He stares at me so intensely that it makes me feel self-conscious about what I'm wearing because I don't know if he's judging my curvy body in this tight leather skirt or if he likes what he sees.

His honey eyes give me a few up-and-downs before turning his attention back to a black-haired female who threads her fingers through his hair. Shivers invade my body as I take in the scene he's displaying for me. He's wearing a shirt almost identical to Hunter's, but it's completely unbuttoned. There's a girl running her hands up and down his chest while another is licking his earlobe. He's got his hands wrapped around the waist of both girls as he sits back and engages in conversation with another male wrestler next to him.

I feel an intense wave of heat violate my core, forcing myself to look away.

Taking another eager glance around the room, I notice the absence of Zayd. It strikes me that maybe he isn't into stuff like this, but then again, who wouldn't be? Hot chicks stroking your ego while you watch strippers dance in front of you. But I'll admit, I am kind of out of my comfort zone.

"Is it actually okay for me to be here?" I ask, looking up at Hunter who seems to have been staring at me the whole time.

Another wave of shivers threatens the surface of my skin as a blush clings to my cheeks.

"What do you mean?" He brushes his fingers—where his hand is still placed on my back—against the fabric of my shirt.

"Conflict of interest, no?" Then again, I didn't know I'd be so close to him when I came. I thought his invite was loose. Like *'hey I'm going to be at this club, so I'll see you there if you go'* kind of thing. Suddenly I feel extremely out of place and my gut is telling me it's time to go. Especially when I see a few of the tall, skinny, and underdressed female wrestlers in the room eyeballing me with what looks like disgust on their faces. Or is that jealousy?

"Don't overthink it, Nova. Come on, let's go dance."

Hunter weaves us through the crowd. I can feel the body heat of everyone we pass to the point where I feel sweat percolate at the top of my eyebrows.

"Can I get you something to drink first?" His question doesn't seem to resonate as being aimed toward me because again, I wasn't expecting to have a personal chauffeur. But the weight of his stare brings me back to attention.

"I'll take a tequila lime, please." I shout over the bass before he leaves me near the middle of the dance floor.

I'm used to sitting on my reading chair with a cup of earl gray tea reading thrillers or watching reruns of The Office. Or maybe the wrestling match that's on that week. I don't get out much. Though I will say, seeing everyone interacting here, engaged in playful conversations or grinding against strangers does give me an adrenaline rush of some sort.

As I scan the masses of club-goers, I recognize a few people from UWE. And then I catch some creep eyeballing me like he's on his deathbed and I'm his last chance at a decent meal. He's wearing a collared button up with very visible armpit stains and a smile that can be confused as pizza grease. His hair is slicked back with that same pizza grease, and I inwardly cringe at the way he licks his lips when he sees me analyzing him back. I turn my head so quickly I almost experience whiplash and my eyes double take on what I see ahead of me.

Dark.

Black.

Irises.

His eyes are searing into my soul as he holds a fragile redhead by the waist, pressed up so close to him that I fear she'll snap in half. He stands nearly a whole foot taller than her as they grind to the hypnotic bump-and-grind song that's taken over the speakers.

He seems to be enjoying himself, but then again, his eyes are eating *me* up. And I jump when he practically tosses the redhead aside and stalks my way. My breathing kicks up to a hundred miles per hour and my heart frantically tries to escape its cavity.

But within almost the same second I can feel him getting closer, Hunter steps into my view with our drinks and I must look like a frightened deer in headlights.

"You okay?" he asks, handing me the tequila lime. I take the glass and look past his shoulder, seeing no sign of Zayden.

He's gone.

Good. Because that man scares the living crap out of me.

But then why do I feel like my vagina is on fire but also, so fucking wet?

"Yeah," I reply before slamming my drink. Not even a wince falls on my face as I take a breath to follow the intake of the smooth liquor. "Let's dance."

Hunter and I are relentless with the way we grind on each other. It's only been about three songs in but I'm feeling the wave of my third tequila course through me. My fingers explore his torso while he grips my hips.

His hands slip lower as a techno-rendition of *Lollipop* echoes through the club, and I can feel his eyes burning into mine when his palms finally slide over the leather skirt on my ass.

Finally.

Despite the proximity and the heat between us, I've been dying for him to risk the adventure of his hands to my ass, needing to feel some kind of friction to accompany the need that is currently embedding itself between my thighs.

"You are so fucking sexy," Hunter whispers darkly in my ear. His soft but buttery rough timber sends ripples of pebbles layering my exposed skin.

"Still think you're annoying," I say back, which earns me a display of the boyish grin that he knows how to flaunt. Though I'm just continuing to give him a hard time, because he really thought he was hot stuff earlier. Honestly, he was. I was so turned on when he semi-forced himself on me in the hallway. But I don't necessarily want him to know that. Because I should have kicked him in his balls. Does he pull that kind of shit often?

Suddenly, he flips me around and plants my ass right into his crotch. His hands are now pressed into the curves above my thighs, the leather tightens as he bends me slightly so as to fit us together better. I can feel his dick start to harden beneath his jeans and my eyes feel heavy at the gesture. I won't survive tonight. But who says I want to.

I'm a grown woman. I'm no stranger to one-night stands either. And despite my rocky start with Hunter, this man knows how to navigate a woman. Should that be a turn off? Some would consider him a player for it. And sure, there are rumors of such, but being the new girl, I can form my own opinion. And my opinion is that Hunter is hot, and I haven't gotten laid in so long. I'd rather it be to someone who might have more of an establishment in the sex department than not.

So . . . *fuck it.*

I grind my ass further into his dick, feeling him grip me harder as his heavy breathing falls into the curve of my neck. I reach a hand up and wrap it behind me to latch my fingers onto his neck. That opens up some room for him to roam one of his hands upward, keeping the other tight in place as we sway lustfully to the next song the DJ whips up.

His venturing hand slides up past the waistband of my skirt, skimming the small sliver of skin showing from my stomach and I swear I hear a light growl come from his mouth and I clench my thighs together on instinct. He makes his way up a little higher, nearly grazing the side of my boob and a small sound escapes my mouth. With how loud it is in here, you'd think no one could hear it. But he did.

Feverishly, he spins me back around and tightens us together.

"I need to get you back to my place, Nova. I'm fucking starving for you." Fuck. I never expected those words to come out of his mouth. Or any man's mouth for that matter. But they graze my cheek in a whisper of need, and I would do anything he asked me to if he used that tone.

But before I open my mouth to answer, the song dying down for the next one to come on and people in the crowd leaving to go get their next drink, I see him again.

Watching.

Zayd stands in the corner leaning against a dark wall. This time, he's alone and his eyes are like daggers as he stares at me.

Why is he always fucking staring at me?

I decide I'm not going to let his mysterious demeanor get to me. Though the ache in my core tightens with so much want. I lean up on my toes, pulling Hunter closer so that my lips barely touch his ears and whisper, "Let's get out of here," while still keeping eye contact with Zayd.

Where this newfound confidence came from? I don't fucking know. I've never been a shy girl by any means but what I just did ranks as the top five boldest moves I've ever made.

And as I weave through the crowd with Hunter's hand in mine, I try to push down the small protest of regret that nags at me.

Regret of what? I'm not quite sure yet. But it isn't loud enough to stop me from enjoying the rest of this night.

WRESTLING

LITTLE STAR

little one

wrestling

Six

NOVA

"You sure you want to do this?" Hunter asks as I unlock the door to my downtown apartment to let us in.

I decided to take him back to my place instead of going to his, because I've only had experience with guys wanting to fuck and be done with me, which is fine. But the walk of shame is actually pretty shameful. This way, I'm not the one who has to leave afterwards. Especially since I know I'll be seeing Hunter around the office.

Gosh, this is so wrong.

But really, I don't care.

I'm needy and honestly, it feels nice to have the attention of someone for once. Like I said, it's been a while.

After my parents died, I had gained a lot of wait. It was gradual but I started to go through phases of eating too much and the stress and depression was really doing its number on me. I mean, sure, I've got perky breasts, and my ass is round and plump—which I love—but I still got made fun of for my weight and it led me to fee self-conscious about myself which in turn, prevented me from being intimate with men. But I developed a deep love for my body over the years. I value my curves and the stretch marks on my thighs and I'm confident in myself. What's that saying? *Thick girls do it better?*

I'm not looking to change the way I look just to please society. No one should have to feel the need for that kind of fuckery. I honestly feel prettier now as a size fourteen than I ever did as a size six, and everyone feels their best at different points in their lives so why should someone's weight matter? Though I'm confident in myself and love the fuck out of my curves, I still get that hint of insecurity when it comes to the stages of undressing during sex.

And even though Hunter has been staring at me the entire two minutes I zoned out like he wants to devour me, I can't help but feel a little self-conscious. This whole situation is intense and so new to me.

"What's on your mind, Nova?" His buttery timber shakes me to my core as I try to come up with a reason as to why I zoned out on him. He's leaning against my front door while I stand in between my kitchen and living room.

My apartment is an open concept, and though it's small, it does what I need it to. But it feels so much smaller knowing that I have someone else in here with me. And hotter too. *Did I leave the heat on?*

"Nova," he reminds me that he asked me a question.

He pushes himself off the door and slowly walks toward me. I don't know where my club-confidence went. But suddenly I'm rendered speechless.

"I just-" I swallow hard when he gets to the point where our feet touch. The smell of mint and tequila spins around my head, reeling from the high it gives me.

"Spit it out, little one." He reaches out to me; his finger grazes my cheeks in a gentle caress. I work hard to not give this man direct eye contact. I can feel myself melting in just his proximity, surprised I survived it at the club.

The memory of his hard cock grinding into my ass is what ultimately provides me the confidence I needed in this moment.

"It's just, it's been so long and I worry that you won't be good enough for me." My words are a sting to his ego, I can tell. And though I said it with a pout and a hint of feigning concern, he knows I meant it in a very bratty, sarcastic way.

"You wanna say that again, Nova?" His response is sharp and just as playful, but I won't lie, it does something different to me. And fuck me, I'm going to hell.

This man is essentially my coworker. Hell, he might even be considered my boss. Or maybe the other way around. I don't know how shit works in the wrestling world when it comes to all that. All I know is that there has to be some kind of rule about crew members fucking one of the wrestling stars but really, who's going to find out?

Just once, right? Just tonight?

"I just really need a man to give me what I need, and I worry that you're not man enough." I'm really playing with fire here, but I can't help it.

And who's to say I'll even remember this is in the morning? I can blame the alcohol on my courageous mockery.

Hunter lowers his hand from my cheek and traces my jawline before resting his grip around my throat.

Then he squeezes. Hard.

I'm so fucking wet.

What kind of girl threatens a man with HR then finds herself choked up in her living room by the same man and gets off on it?

I don't know what's happening or how we got here, but I'd be lying if I said I wasn't so turned on right now.

"When I had you pinned against the wall earlier today, I knew your little prim and proper was just an act. I knew that deep down there was this naughty little brat waiting to be taken care of, Nova. That's what attracted me to you." He leans down to the crook of my neck and inhales deep as he squeezes just a little tighter, the threat of passing out is a real possibility right now. But the strength of his grip on my throat only deepens the pool of lust swirling between my thighs.

"I will show you what kind of man can handle a woman like you, little one." I can't do anything but let out a little whimper which sounds more like a pornographic moan than a protest of fear. And honestly, I don't know which I intended because I *am* scared but the liquid heat dripping down my thighs betrays me.

And I started this.

I didn't tell him to back off in the hallway.

I accepted his invitation to the club.

I let him fit us together while we danced, like two puzzle pieces to complete the final image.

And I egged him on just now, intentionally. I wanted to get a rise out of him, to see how far I could go with him.

Because I want this. Despite what my head is telling me is right, I *need* this.

He lets go of the grip he has around my neck, and I gasp, needing air more than I need anything else right now.

But his feverish glare about knocks me on my ass.

"I want you on the bed, Nova. All fours."

"You . . . what?" I stutter, because what the hell? *All fours?* What kind of *Animal Planet* shit is this man into?

Okay, so maybe this isn't all that crazy, but I can confirm I've never had anyone choke me, first of all, and then demand me to get on all fours. So let me just reel in my vacillation between whether this is degrading or scorchingly hot.

"Now," he demands, but his tone doesn't express aggression as much as it gives off desire. So I listen to him.

I walk over to the bed and lean up on it. I feel comfort slip away as I lean over and steady myself on my hands and knees, facing the headboard. The leather skirt sits extremely tight, and I can feel air creep between my thighs confirming that it's short enough that he can see my ass.

"Fuck." I hear him say and he comes closer.

I shift a little, not really knowing how long I have to stay like this, but I hear his steps approach the bed and I can't help but feel a little giddy.

I feel his hands touch the back of my thighs. The heat burns its way to my center as he gradually and intimately drags his fingers up toward the curve of my ass. Goosebumps cover my skin as I'm sure he can see. I dip my head and close my eyes, imagining him doing exactly what he's doing, what he's seeing. My heart is heavy in my chest as it pounds against its restraint, and I can feel my arousal literally dripping down my thighs.

"You're so fucking sexy, little one. Let's get you out of this skirt." I attempt to move from my position, expecting to get up and strip myself but in a matter of seconds, I hear the tough tear of fabric rip through my leather skirt and suddenly, the item of clothing is pulled from my body seamlessly.

My gasp is loud and breathy. And I can feel his smirk all the way to my soul.

"Did you just-" Nerves wrack my body as the action of him ripping off my skirt—my leather fucking skirt, just ripped down the seam—sends painful need to my core. "That was an expensive skirt," I say, not knowing how else to react or what else to say, still on all fours.

"I'll buy you another one, Nova. Besides, it looks better on the floor."

Oh. My. God.

Is this really happening? Is this real life? Am I about to actually do this?

Something foreign stirs deep in my throat and tickles its way down to low in my belly, only heightened when I Hunter smacks my ass.

That hurt.

But I like it.

So much so that I find myself pushing my ass back hoping for more.

"Such an eager little brat aren't you, Nova?" Hunter's voice vibrates through me like a tsunami, and I moan with such need.

"Please." I find myself begging. Which shocks the hell out of me. I've never begged for anything in my entire life.

I feel the straps of my thong being slid down my ass and toward my thigh, surprised that he's taking such gentle care of that as opposed to what he did to my skirt.

"Lift your knees for me," he directs, and I do so that he can discard my thong somewhere on the floor.

My oversized t-shirt is still covering the top of me, and I pray to whoever is in charge that he doesn't try to rip it from my body. I really like this shirt.

I don't see much of what he's doing. My eyes are closed, and my head dipped between my shoulders as I struggle to stay up on my knees. Not because I'm weak, but because my need for him to touch me is making me shake.

He smacks my ass again. And I almost buckle in my position because of how hard it was. That's definitely going to bruise.

"Scoot up on the bed a little bit, little one." I inch up a tad toward the headboard and look behind my shoulders to see him just casually sliding underneath me, his face lining up with my pussy.

"What are you doing?" I ask, when clearly, I know what he's doing. But I don't believe it.

"I can see that you're dripping, Nova. Want me to take care of this sweet little pussy for you?" I feel his fingers graze the lips of my pussy before he spreads me open.

Hunter doesn't wait for me to answer before his finger enters my pussy. I moan almost embarrassingly but I can't help that he wrings that out of me.

"I can take care of it for you, Nova. But if you don't think I'm man enough..." he trails off as he removes his finger and I protest. Vocally.

"No, please. You're man enough. Hunter, please." I am nearly whining from how painfully I feel the need, begging with no shame. He can't bring me this close just to edge me and leave me wanting. I'd rather be doing a walk of shame tomorrow than have my night end like that.

"That's what I thought, little one. Sit up. Hands on the headboard." As I release some of the weight from my knees, I scoot up a little bit closer to gain a better hold of the headboard. Simultaneously, I hear my phone buzz. It's only a text. So, I let it go. Nothing is more important than this right now, selfishly.

"Don't hold back on me, okay, Nova? I want your legs shaking for me, baby. Let me hear how good I make you feel." Hunter's voice is so close to my pussy as he talks to me. I look down and I can barely see his bright blues buried beneath me. I shiver at the sight as I grip the top of my headboard tightly.

I almost forget that we're in my room. The curtains to my window are shut and the lights are dimmed. I look over to my left and I realize I can see the position we're in clear as day in the mirrors that are plastered on the doors of my closet. Chills wrack my body when I see how scandalous this looks, how *dirty*. I've never been in this position before. And I-

"Oh my god!" I yelp when I feel Hunter's tongue trace my seam. I almost faint from how fucking good it feels. His tongue slides over my clit and I swear I'm already about to come.

A low growl rumbles from Hunter's voice as he continues his assault on my wanton pussy. He licks and sucks and draws out the lustiest moans from my mouth, even *I'm* surprised. I can't think straight. I don't want to. If I knew his mouth felt like this, I'd have let him take me in the hallway.

I find myself rocking against his mouth and his fingertips dig into the flesh of my ass.

"Right there!" I nearly squeal. And I'm rewarded with two fingers for it, he must have really liked me vocalizing my needs.

"Hunter!" I moan.

"Come on, little one. You can do better than that. Ride me." And I do. I look into the mirror and see this man's fingers entering me and leaving me. Thrusting as I grind against his face. I don't realize that I push some of my weight down on him, nearly suffocating the man and when I go to ease up, he digs his fingers into the flesh of my thighs in a harsh protest and brings me down further.

"Fuck," I whisper, and I feel the wave of my orgasm rippling through me. "I'm going to come, Hunter. I-oh fuck!" He doesn't relent the motion of his fingers, instead he curls them deeper and steadies his tongue over my clit, sucking and pulling.

I'm nearly crying because it feels so fucking good. I grind hard against his face as my orgasm rips through me and I feel my pussy clenching around his fingers. His groans only heighten my release of pleasure and when I feel like I can breathe again, I let go of the headboard, realizing that my knuckles were white from holding on so tightly.

"Holy shit," I say mainly to myself, but Hunter hears me.

"Did that do it for you, little one?" I'm breathing quickly, trying to catch my breath as Hunter slides out from underneath me.

All I do is nod and let out a whiny little whimper to hopefully indicate that it did in fact do it for me.

I turn around and rest my back against the headboard, Hunter leans against the bed, his hands pushed into the mattress as he stares at me like he's deprived of water.

"You're so fucking pretty with my mouth on your pussy, Nova. But I want to see what you look like with your mouth full of my cock."

Seven

Hunter

She's laying at the head of her bed, her pussy glistening in the dim light still wet from her orgasm and the literal tongue lashing I just gave it. I swear I've never tasted pussy so good. And her cheeks wear the color pink so prettily when I tell her what I want to do next. It's been fun watching her open up to me in the last twelve hours.

Though my intention wasn't to do what I did back at headquarters earlier, I couldn't resist. It was instinct, believe it or not. She was pulling me in, and I wanted to push the limits.

She played it off at first, but she eventually broke at the club. Again, my intention was not to end up here with her. At least not tonight. I genuinely wanted to get to know her.

She stares back at me in utter amazement and nearly sedated from the orgasm her body expelled, coming undone on my tongue. I don't blame her. And man, she rode me like her life depended on it. Like she hadn't been eaten in quite some time.

And that makes my dick so fucking hard.

I eye her up, her thick voluptuous thighs, spread just enough for me to see what's between. The taste of her cum still lingering in my mouth. I can tell she was a little uncomfortable with the idea that she'd be fully naked in front of me, she probably thinks her curves will scare me away but I'm not a little boy. And I crave to see what she's hiding underneath her shirt, but I'll let her keep it on for now because I want to ease her into being comfortable with undressing in front of me. But I promise I'm going to cherish the fuck out of her entire body when she grants me access on her own accord.

For now. I'll enjoy the view she allows, and I can't wait to feel her pretty mouth wrap around my dick.

"You better hurry and show me what you're working with, Hunter, because I'm getting tired," she quips. That sassy shit she talks to me really gets me going. She's being a brat on purpose, and I like that she hits these peaks of confidence and knows just the right time to swing 'em at me. Fuck, she turns me on.

"Crawl to me, little one. Unzip my pants for me." I love that she takes my direction well. And I love that it turns her on. The little shiver her body gives is the proof. And that makes me a very satisfied man.

She gets back on all fours and even though there's hardly any space from where she's at to where I am, she still does what she's told.

Fuck, my dick is straining in my jeans. I don't think I've been this hard in a while. I watch her crawl toward the end of the bed, meeting my gaze with her own hazel eyes, basically chewing on her bottom lip as she comes closer.

"Such a good fucking girl, Nova," I praise her when she reaches the edge. She unzips my jeans just like I had asked her, and I reach in and pull my dick out.

It bobs just inches from her face and the hitch in her breath makes it throb. I'm so fucking hard.

"I want you to lay down on your back. But I want your head right here on the edge of the bed. And spread your legs, little one."

She does exactly what I say. Her tits bounce under her shirt as she settles on her back, and I nearly rip it off her just to see what's underneath, but I promised myself I'd let her keep it on until she wanted to take it off herself.

I slip my jeans and boxers all the way down to my ankles as I watch my good girl get situated under me. I'm leaning over her slightly as her head teeters the edge of the bed. I stroke myself above her and I can see the clench she's trying to hide in her thighs.

"I'm going to fuck your mouth now, little one. If it's too hard, pinch my thighs. But I know you can take it." I position my dick over her mouth, open and waiting for me.

Fuck, she's perfect. I knew it when I saw her for the first time when Shawn introduced her. I know the other guys felt it too and I can't lie, I'm fucking reeling that I got to her first. Again, not that the intention was to get her like this, or maybe it was. But I also want to show her that I can take care of her.

Don't ask me why I feel that way because I've known the girl for less than a day, but I guess when you know, you know. Not that I plan to fall in love or get married right away but I swear there's something clawing at me that tells me I'm gonna want to keep her around for a while.

She pushes herself a little further toward the edge to tilt her head back off of the bed as I put the tip of it against her lips so that her throat is wide open for me—nearly hanging upside down—and I smile at the fucking gesture.

"You are so fucking beautiful, Nova. Let's see how well you take my dick." I press past her lips; her tongue greets me sweetly in a swirl of greed as I press myself further into her mouth.

She reaches up and grabs the base of my cock, realizing she won't be able to take all of me. I can see her chest rise and fall as she slides her hand up and down to accompany her mouth as I work my way as far as I can before she lets out a gagged moan.

Her legs fall open a little wider, so I reach over and pinch her clit with my finger which garners the sexiest sound from her. I almost blow my load right then, but I lean over her body and focus on thrusting my dick into her mouth.

She coats me with her saliva, working me with one hand while she sucks me into her mouth. I feel the slight graze of teeth scrape against my sensitive skin and her gargled sounds of sucking me off becomes all I can focus on, and it makes me push harder. She arches her back off the bed and I gather that she likes it a little rough.

I lean down to her pussy, spread her lips open to me and press a kiss to her clit before sucking on her ball of nerves completely. We're like this for about a minute when I feel my release approaching.

I decide I'm going to play a little game with her since she wanted to cop an attitude with me earlier.

"I'm going to push myself as far as I can against the back of your throat, Nova. I won't thrust, I won't move.

Until you make yourself come. Then I'm going to come down your throat and I need you to swallow all of me. Understand?"

I remove my dick from her mouth, my balls grazing her forehead and I can feel them tighten at the friction it provides. A string of her saliva leads from her mouth to my dick, and I just can't get enough of what this girl does to me.

"Yes, daddy," she whispers and my fucking dick surges, my release nearly pummeling through me but I have to stop it. She can tell I'm already so fucking close.

Daddy.

So, she makes quick work of her pussy while I push my cock as deep as I can against the back of her throat. It's harder for me not to move or come too soon as she swallows against the tip of my dick, and I watch her finger herself.

I might come before she does.

Her finger flicks at her clit before she dips it to her entrance and slides in. A moan vibrates around my cock and I know she can feel the pulse from my cock so she works faster. I feel her writhe beneath me at the same time her stomach tightens and her legs start to shake. I am pressing so hard against her throat, haven't moved the slightest as she holds me like a pro but I can tell she's struggling to breathe and she's starting to gag. But she knows the rules.

And just like that, she starts to cry and moan with her mouth full of my cock, convulsing around her fingers as her orgasm tears through her. The vibrations of her moans travel all the way to my balls and I take this moment to finally thrust my cock out of her throat only to slide back in. Tears escape her eyes as she gags while she comes and I finally release my cum into her tight little mouth.

"Fuck, fuck, fuck," I chant. She's an angel to my sinful prayers, this little one. She finishes coming and grabs the base of my cock while she swallows the last drop of my cum.

I pull myself out of her mouth and she gasps for air desperately as cum and saliva coat her lips. I've never come so hard in my life.

I lift her up gently into a sitting position and head into her kitchen for a glass of water. I meet her back at the bed and she's still panting. I sit next to her and hand her the glass. She sips from it eagerly and I pet her back, smoothing her hair back into place.

"Did I hurt you?" I ask her, fearing that she was just trying to impress me instead of tapping out.

She finishes the water and leans over to set the cup on her nightstand. The time on the clock reads just after midnight. Shawn won't like that I'm out past curfew. Yes, we professional wrestlers annoyingly have a curfew.

Nova reaches her hand out to wipe the lone tear trailing down her cheek from one of her eyes before answering me, "Yes, you did." My heart drops a little. Now that definitely wasn't supposed to happen.

But the girl stuns me, shocks me to my core when she leans forward, wrapping her fingers around the side of my neck to bring my ear closer to her lips and whispers, "But I liked it."

Eight

NOVA

I turn over in my bed, seeing the morning light peek through my sheer white curtains. My apartment sits higher up, and I can tell the sun is fully ablaze. I reach over to grab my phone to check the time but my eyes bulge at the missed email from Shawn earlier this morning and I see that I've got an unread text from last night.

"Shit!" I shout to myself, seeing that the email is a notice of a mandatory meeting for ten o'clock which is in...thirty fucking minutes.

I turn to see that Hunter is not in bed with me. He must have left earlier this morning.

After everything that we did last night, I was exhausted and ended up falling asleep in Hunter's arms surprisingly.

I feel heat burn my cheeks at just the thought of how good he made me feel. I look down and see that I'm still only wearing my bra and t-shirt and I blush relentlessly at how he allowed me to show him only with what I felt comfortable with. But it's not that I wasn't comfortable or confident with him, it's just that he provided me with so much attention even only being half naked that the rest of the undressing part skipped my mind.

He gave me the attention I've been dying to have. Attention I never got from any other man, and he praised me while I cried out his name. When I listened to him, I was his good girl. And my whole body ignited with the recognition he gave me.

It was . . . liberating.

I remember I have an unread text so before I rummage through my closet for something to wear and bury my honey hair into a parade of dry shampoo, I open it.

> I don't like seeing another man's hands on you, Nova. You get three strikes before I decide to discipline you for your disobedience.

The message comes from an unknown phone number and as much as I want to think about what the fuck this message means, I don't have time. Besides, someone is probably just fucking with me, and I don't want to think too deeply about this. But I'd be lying if I said I wasn't concerned about the fact that someone might be watching me and saw me come home with Hunter.

But then another text shoots through from the same number.

> Strike 1.

Is all it reads, and I roll my eyes at the attempted mystery the sender is trying to convey. Or fear. Or both. But I don't have time to think about it any further. I need to get my ass to the office before I'm fired.

This definitely can't happen again.

"You're late, Miss Satterlee," Shawn announces loudly as I walk into the meeting room. All eyes are on me and I hope to God they don't notice my sex-flushed face. Though it's been hours since Hunter and I messed around, and we didn't *actually* fuck.

But I shake the thought and put on my best professional face as I apologize to the meeting attendees such as my boss and a few of the crew members like stage managers, writers, and some of the commentators, and I take my seat next to one of the only other girls in the room.

"As I was saying," Shawn continues once I'm seated in my chair, "We're going to need something fresh this week that no one will see coming. We need an op for Zayd and we need to make it TV worthy or we will lose our ranking for live television and we lose our reputation in the business." He stops his statement and takes a look around, whispers of chatter echo throughout the room and I mentally berate myself for being late as I clearly missed something.

"I'm sorry," I say. My voice is on the verge of trembling as I wonder if I'm even allowed to speak up, but I change gears and decide to ask my question pointedly and with lack of shyness.

Everyone points their eyes in my direction.

"Again. Apologies for being late, but am I missing something here? Isn't Zayden slated to fight The Irish Hero?" I make sure I'm sitting as straight as I can and that my eyes are talking louder than my voice. I want them to take me seriously even though I clearly can't be trusted to be on time.

"Gryffin got arrested last night, for real. He threw a bottle of something at a bartender for denying him any more drinks. He's not going to be able to make it to the show on Friday," Shawn sighs an annoyed puff of air, probably more annoyed at me than at Gryffin.

"I think we can paint a storyline that indicates that Gryffin chickened out of the match." Someone with cropped, blue hair and thick, black frames speaks up.

"What's your name?" I decide to ask, realizing I don't know many of the people I'm supposed to be working with.

"Name's Chris, they/them. I'm the script editor for the writing team." They give me a brief smile and nod my way.

"Chris, don't you think the paparazzi would be all over this by now. You can't really create a false storyline unless it includes his arrest. But let's be honest, the media outlets are probably typing up their reports as we speak." I look around at some of the other members to try and gauge their apprehension of my comment and they all seem to be pretty satisfied.

"You're right," Chris admits, their eyes drawing toward their notepad as they cross out one of the bullet points listed on it.

"So then what would you suggest, Nova?" I turn to look at the man who responded to me.

I know this person, his name is Darnel and he's the head of the creative writing team. I've dreamed of working for him and now that I'm finally here and he's asking me about my thoughts, I almost choke.

He stares at me in anticipation. His dark brown eyes match his beautifully dark skin and though I've seen his beautiful bright smile before—thanks to the behind the scenes videos I researched—he's not showing it off right now, expressing serious interest in what I have to say.

He's the most talented man in this business, probably even more so than the actual wrestlers because he's the one who creates the stories behind each match, with the help of his writing team of course. But his mind works in different ways and he's asking me, Nova Satterlee, what I would suggest to help turn this change of events around.

I sit up a little straighter in my chair and mentally prepare myself for what an honor it is to even be giving him my ideas.

"Well, first. I think we say that Gryffin put on a big show at the bar last night knowing that it would get him in trouble only to purposefully get himself out of the match because he was afraid of losing to Zayden. I know that might do a little bit of damage to his Irish Hero persona, but I think it could be good later down the road. We might even be able to spin it to make him the perfect heel later on. Viewers eat that shit up." I choke a bit on my use of curse words but I can't help it when my fangirl comes out sometimes, especially when talking about wrestling. I notice the slightest looks of horror as I continue with my idea.

"Zayd is angry now, right? I mean, he's already the villain but why not heighten that evil and pair it with another set of evil. He's pissed that Gryffin took the easy way out. Insert the tag-team match. We can merge the main event and the tag-team match together. We can have Zayd interrupt the match toward the end. He runs down the ramp to the stage, throws himself into the ring in the middle of the match and takes his anger out on the UKO brothers." I pause to give them time to process this as I see some of the writers writing notes down and even Shawn looks intrigued.

"Gryffin and the UKO brothers have somewhat of a friendship in this business, and all we have to do is convince the viewers that the UKO brothers put Gryffin up to his antics as some kind of drunken dare and the result is Zayd raging on the tag-team match and joining Hunter and Krew in their quest to defeat the brothers. And of course..." I trail off, waiting to see if someone will pick up what I'm dropping.

"Always the champion, never the hero." I look over to see that Chris said exactly what I was thinking.

"Zayd gets to keep his heavyweight championship belt, Hunter and Krew keep their tag-team champion title but we've also just created the deadliest trio in the business since *the attitude era.*" I refer to an older time of the UWE and that garners the full attention of everyone in the meeting room.

I feel an ounce of accomplishment wash over me as I finally see Darnel's smirk revealing his pearly whites.

"Where did you find this girl?" He turns to ask Shawn and he decides to use that moment to talk about how close he and my father were. Which cannot be further from the truth. I know he was around my father back in the day when Shawn's dad, Victor, ran things, but my dad never really liked either man.

Then again, who did my dad like?

But I let him continue with his false stories of whatever bullshit he's spewing because I don't want to think or talk about my father right now.

"I like it," Darnel turns to me as if he didn't hear a single word come out of Shawn's mouth and acknowledges my idea.

"Can you fine-tune everything Nova just said and get it to script before tomorrow night? We have less than twenty-four hours to get this story line in full blanket mode." Darnel looks over to his writing team partners and they all nod, each of them writing something down before getting up to leave.

"We'll need to inform Zayd of the change to his character storyline asap," Shawn chimes in.

"I'll tell him," I offer almost desperately. I don't know what possesses me to do so, but my mouth was blurting eagerly before my brain could shut it down.

"Umm, sure. Just find him and tell him to meet with the writing crew." Shawn gives me a confusing onceover but I don't let it linger before I pack up my own stuff to head out.

But before I make it too far, someone taps on my shoulder.

"It was Hunter wasn't it?" I turn to see that the woman I was sitting next to is now behind me and the question catches me off guard.

She's pretty. Really pretty. She has long dark, stick straight hair and green eyes that scream against her pale skin. She's only a few inches taller than me and her thin smile reaches her ears as she waits for me to answer her,

"I'm sorry?" I ask, moving out of the way as everyone filters out of the meeting room leaving only the two of us left.

"Don't think I can't tell when a girl's been puttin' in work all night, sweetie." She giggles and heat rises to my cheeks. That's when I realize that I recognize her from the club last night. She was one of the girls that was all over Krew.

"Don't worry, your secret's safe with me." She smirks before she walks away.

That was . . . weird.

But I push on to my next mission which, just thinking about it, sends appetitive chills down my spine.

I've got to go find Zayden Stone.

Nine

NOVA

As I walk down the back hallways, I get a sense of Deja vu. Images of Hunter pressing me up against the cold concrete with his annoyingly hot body flash through my head incredulously. I try to push them down knowing that I have a job to do, and I can't let that happen again.

But just as if his ears were ringing, I get a text from the man.

> Sorry I had to leave so early. Had to prepare for when Bossman ripped me for missing curfew. But I really Enjoyed last night. I'd love to do it again.

Reading his message makes me smile, but really, we *can't* do it again. We *shouldn't* do it again.

But I *want* to do it again.

I have to admit that I feel rather satisfied after last night and I really did enjoy the thrill it gave me. But God, if I had any common sense or decency at all I'd look at my slutty self and tell her to get her shit together.

So, I feign a moment of self-control and look up and down the hall for the training room. That's where I was told I'd find Zayd.

I type out a response to Hunter and send it on its way.

> Sounds good.

But I instantly regret the open door of possibilities I just stupidly conveyed when I know I should have just turned him down nicely. But how do you say no to something that makes you feel so good? Besides, it's not a promise of marriage, just an invitation for some more pillow talk . . . minus the talking.

I finally approach a door that says TRAINING on it and then I realize there are four more just like it down the hall. I walk up to the one right in front of me and attempt to open it, but it's locked. So I move on to the next one which opens up to a mini gym, but the lights are off, and no one is inside.

I walk down to the third door and pause to the throaty sound of a man grunting. He *has* to be in this room. I approach the door and open it gently so as to not scare him and force him to drop a weight down on himself, but when I open the door a sliver, a man lifting weights is not what my eyes have front seat to.

Female moans accompany the groans that I heard, and I focus on what I'm watching, not really intending to be nosey but the provocative display in front of me is intriguing.

There's a raven-haired female tied to the pullup bar and her feet aren't even touching the ground. Instead, they're wrapped around the rock-hard shoulders of a man. My heart sinks in a freefall of jealousy when I recognize who this is.

It's Krew.

But jealous of what? I'm not sure. I've never even spoken to the man for me to feel that form of betrayal or envy of the woman he's got his tongue on. And I can tell she's enjoying herself as he eats her out while she's hanging from her wrists, bound by some kind of rope.

Krew Rivers is devouring this woman, and the pang of jealousy turns to desire as I see the perfect O form over her lips and she writhes in his grip. The sounds he's pulling from her turns me on in ways I never thought possible.

Krew is only wearing his gym shorts, his devilishly sexy calves on full display with more tattoos. His dark brown curls hang down his back while he continues his feast on this girl's pussy.

I lean in slightly to the door, desperate to see more and that's when I notice her face.

It's the girl from the meeting, and the one from the club last night.

So this is what she ran off to do?

Fuck around in the training room with Krew? Do they do this often?

"Fuck, right there, Krew." Her breathy cries bring heat to my cheeks as I think of my own cries of rapture from the night before, compliments of Hunter Dodge.

God, *this is so wrong*.

But before I can step out and walk away, my phone buzzes in my hand which shocks the hell out of me, sending me bumping into the door and making the biggest fucking scene possibly imaginable.

Embarrassment shatters across my face as I look up and see that Krew and his tied-up companion are staring at me in nothing other than a casual curiosity.

"Oh, please don't stop my account. I was just looking for someone and obviously he's not here so I'm just gonna go now." I hide my eyes with my hand like I'm trying to block out the sun, feeling more shame than ever before.

I turn to leave the way I came but I'm interrupted before I can exit.

"Shut the door, sweetheart." Krew's raspy timbre shakes me to my core. I've heard him speak before, sure. But not in the same room as me and definitely not with the juices of another woman's pussy glistening on his lips. It's a nefarious sight.

"Yes, I plan to. Sorry again." I wave my hand awkwardly and attempt one last time to turn and walk away.

But I freeze when I hear heavy footsteps eat up the space behind me and I steady my hand on the doorknob. I feel him right behind me as he reaches over and closes the door leaving me *in* the room instead of out of it. I feel his hand graze my arm when he reels it back in and walks back over to the girl still dangling from the pullup bar. I see her on full display and something warm creeps under my skin when I take in the image of what I'm seeing.

Is she okay being watched like that?

Does she like it?

Would I like it?

My shoulders drop in confusion, realizing I was tense.

Sooo . . . am I supposed to just watch?

Krew starts fitting himself back in between her legs, lifting her up as to relieve the rope from digging into her skin. I'm surprised they held her like that for so long.

I have no time to fucking think about what the hell is happening because it seems like Krew unleashes a tornado on this poor lady as she screams and cries in so much pleasure that she bucks harshly against his face. I'm forced to stand here and watch her get obliterated by this man's mouth; she wiggles intensely against the restraints holding her up.

I mean, I can still turn around and leave. I'm not really *forced* to stay. Just because he marched over here all macho-man doesn't mean I'm bound to this room. But part of me *wants* to stay. Part of me wants to watch what he wants me to watch.

The bind that holds the girl to the bar starts to unravel and in the same moment, her orgasm reaches her. Her eyes close tightly and her moans turn to prayers to God. The only thing holding her up now is Krew's grip on her ass and her legs wrapped around his shoulder.

I'm so forbiddingly turned on that it hurts. Watching him bring her to her point of pleasure like this sends jolts of thrill tingling to my core and the need to touch myself, or be touched, is strong.

I look down to the ground to try and bury my own enjoyment from what I'm witnessing but then I hear her moans die down and I see that he's letting her down to her feet. I turn around as if to give her privacy but that seems pretty fucking silly considering I was just gifted the VIP ticket to this exhilarating performance, watching her come on Krew's mouth while tied up.

But, Jesus, it turned me on.

Suddenly, I hear smaller footsteps approach and I curiously look over to see the raven-haired girl coming into view only to stop before opening the door to say, "Have fun." She winks at me before opening the door, exiting, and then closing the door.

Still in this room.

Still with Krew.

"I'm just gonna follow-" I attempt to say, not quite sure why I would need to stay behind or why he insisted I stay in the first place but before I can escape, he's charging toward me.

He approaches so fast that I fall back into the door, palms flail out to the sides of me, pressing into the door to hold me as he pins me on either side of my head.

He's got me caged in, almost how Hunter did yesterday. But his stare is much fiercer as he looks down at me from his tall stature. His dark brown eyes glare at me.

"I didn't say you could leave, sweetheart." What the fuck is with these men? Do they really think that they can force themselves on girls like this and that we'll just let them do whatever they fuck they want?

Oh, what am I saying? Of course, they do. And I'm walking proof seeing as I let one of them do just that to me no less than twenty-four hours ago.

"I was looking for Zayden. You, umm . . . wouldn't happen to know where he is, would you?" I'm practically a mess of nerves and fear as Krew towers over me. He's all looming and dark while I cower like a baby beneath him.

His heady scent of leather mixed with sweat latches on to my senses and renders me completely enthralled.

"No." Is all he says and the way his voice shakes creates a fear in me that I want to actually enjoy feeling. Like the fright of what he might do to me turns me on, oddly enough.

But I can't hide the way my body is trembling with so much need right now, and I want him to make it go away.

We stay like this for what seems like hours but really is only about two minutes. Just him breathing down on me like he owns me and little ole me just fighting for my portion of air. But I'm helpless under his possession, caged between his arms like an animal. *But I like it.*

"Can I plea-" I try to beg for him to release me so that I can make an exit. I was doing a fabulous job earlier, actually making some headway in the new career path but this was not on the agenda for today.

But I can't even complete a full sentence without him interrupting me.

"Can you what, sweetheart?" His lips barely open when he speaks to me which kind of drives me crazy because I just want to scream, and he's being so quiet while his husky tone presents power.

I zone out on his body, roaming over every hard outline of his chest and his neck and his shoulders and his abs. My breathing becomes painfully impossible to keep up with. I'm hot and so fucking bothered.

"Nova."

"Oh, umm..." I think about what he asked me but I'm too lost in the way he exudes dominance. What do I want? And the answer to that could come from a million different things. Because though I was going to ask if he'd let me leave, and I really do think he'd let me if I asked, there's something I want more.

I feel myself tense up knowing that I'm about to say what my brain is telling to avoid confessing but I can't help it. The feeling is too strong and I know he'll give it to me if I ask.

"I want to come," I whisper so lightly that it sounds like a questionable prayer to someone or something I'm not sure exists.

I mean, what woman in their right mind would think to tell a man that she wants to come?

"Good girl," he growls and nods over to the benches. I don't argue or fight it, I simply walk where he told me to, like I'm brainwashed, and sit on the barbell bench.

Adrenaline kicks up at what might happen next. What *do* I want to happen next?

He simply smirks at me, the force of how dirty it is knocks me on my ass, because he can see my lack of resolve painted all over my face.

I look up at him behind my hooded eyes. I feel it all the way to my toes. The lust. The need. The desire.

But I also feel ashamed. I just watched him eat another girl out, shouldn't that concern me? Turn me off even? Though, I know that's not how I feel, and I know that I shouldn't actually be ashamed of it. And something about the way Krew is looking at me puts me at ease, even though it's all possessive and dark.

"What are you gonna do to me?" I ask, feeling so much anxiety from the silence that was permeating.

"I'm gonna give you what you want, Nova. I'm gonna make you come," he states in a low tone as he points to my shirt. "Off."

I look down in confusion, though I know what he wants. He wants me to unbutton my silk blouse and discard it.

"I should really get-" I start to deny his demand, feeling a tightness cord through my lungs and branch out into tickles that spread all over my skin like wildfire. It's too much. But he avoids my attempt at a protest.

"I wasn't asking, Nova. Now, take it off or I do it for you." Krew always gave me butterflies whenever I watched him perform on TV. But nothing compares to having him stand so close to me in real life. I feel it everywhere. It's hot in here, and if only to get some reprieve, I start to unbutton my shirt. But I'm shaky. Out of excitement or concern for my well-being, I'm not sure yet. But obviously I'm too hesitant for Krew's liking because he reaches down and yanks my top right off my body. Buttons smack the floor and the tear of fabric rips through the room.

Fuck.

He rips my shirt in two just as he does to his every time he wrestles on stage.

My breath hitches when he lifts me up aggressively—and with absolute ease—taking me by the back of my thighs and pressing my core to his torso tight as he walks us into the wall behind the bench.

The pain from my back smacking the wall starts immediately but then it fades when he digs his mouth into the curve of my neck and kisses me there fiercely.

The initiative of this man knocks me senseless and has me dizzy with exhilaration.

Moaning softly at first, I grind into him. Then I get a little excited and start getting louder when his mouth trails past my collarbone to the curve of my breast.

He pulls down the cup of my black lace bra and doesn't waste any time taking a nipple into his hot, wet mouth.

It feels like a fever dream. There's no way this is really happening. And I'm already so flustered that I feel like I might black out, or maybe it's from the intense pleasure that I'm feeling.

His fingers dig into my jean-clad ass as he presses me harder into the wall, like he's desperate to taste me deeper, still swirling his tongue over the hardened peak of my breast.

I don't know what to do with my hands. I press them against the wall behind me, nervous he'll drop me. Then I dig them into his hair then run them down over his shaved scalp, feeling like velvet.

"Fuck Nova, you are intoxicating," he says before moving over to my next breast. I moan at his praise, but I jump when I hear my phone vibrating on the concrete floor by the door. I must have dropped it when Krew crowded me earlier.

"I should . . . oh god . . . I should get that," I whimper when he lets my nipple go with a harsh *pop*.

He sets me down on my feet and walks over to my phone.

My heart races intrepidly when I see him look at who's calling, then looking right into my eyes, he answers the call.

"Yes?" His glare is overwhelming, and I just allow this man to answer my phone for me, still not knowing who it could be.

"Training room number 3." Then he hangs up.

"Umm, who was that?" I ask, feeling an ounce of awkwardness seep into the atmosphere. I attempt to pull my bra back on but he stops me.

"Don't. I want to see your tits bounce while I fuck you, Nova."

Holy shit. What did he just say to me?

My cheeks burn with desire as my whole body ignites with need. I let my bra go, reaching around to undo it entirely, not really sure why I do but everything is so tense and sexual tension charges through the air. It drops to the floor and the look of satisfaction that rolls over his face sends chills down my spine.

It's an audacious move for sure. I guess you can say I'm feeling rather adventurous in this moment.

"I saw the look of adoration in your eyes earlier, sweetheart. You liked watching me with Reyna earlier. You liked watching me eat out her pussy while she came on my tongue. Didn't you?" He presses his body into mine while he runs his fingers through my tousled hair.

I can't escape his hold, and I don't want to. And even though he just ignored my question again, I nod at him as a little whimper leaves my mouth.

"But even more, I can tell that you wanted to know what it would be like to be watched. Isn't that right?" Krew is towering over me, his shadow closing me in and forcing me to take in every inch of his hard dick pressed against my stomach.

I feel his fingers trail from my shoulders and down the side of my arm. Then back up and over my breast before circling over my nipples.

I buck gently, needing to feel his fingers in other places.

I attempt to unbutton my jeans. I need them off now. My body feels constricted as the tight denim digs into my skin.

"No. I want him to watch." He places his hand over my own to stop me from going further.

"Who's him?" I ask curiously and maybe even worriedly. Who was on the phone?

But speak of the devil, Hunter opens the door to the room and casually walks inside before shutting us all back in.

"There she is," he whispers. And while his tone is soft compared to Krew's low rasp, it's still infuriatingly sexy. "I came for the show, Nova. I hope you don't mind."

Butterflies assault my tummy as I look between the two men in front of me. Hunter is attractive as hell with his school-boy smile and his daring blue eyes while Krew parades his dark features and ink-etched body considerably well.

And I can't help but succumb to the ripple of need that washes over my body. Both of these men have their eyes on me, and I almost forget that I'm topless as I notice my bra and shreds of my shirt are scattered across the floor. Still dressed in my jeans, the one thing I need to get out of desperately.

"I didn't get to see this part of you last night." He walks my way. "May I?" he asks, but he wasn't asking me. He was asking . . . Krew?

Krew nods his head and focuses his eyes on the movements of Hunter who closes the gap between us and looks at me dead in my eyes.

"I didn't expect for you to move on so quickly, little one," he whispers in my ear, but I don't sense betrayal lacing his tone. Instead, I sense the opposite. He braces himself against the wall behind me, placing one hand on each side of my head flat against the surface.

"Good thing I don't mind sharing."

WRESTLING

LITTLE STAR

little one

Ten

KREW

She's going to take us both so well. I can tell she's never done anything like this before, but she deserves to be fucking treasured. And the look on her face is pure angst as she waits for one of us to tell her what's about to happen next.

Hunter stands in the corner a few feet over and watches as our pretty little plaything takes deep breaths, trying to suppress her lust for this moment. And my, does she look beautiful while flushed and hot.

When she first got introduced to us, Hunter whispered something to me about the way her body looked in that dress she was in. And while I didn't really hear what he said to me, I knew that once Hunter had his eyes on something, there was no getting in his way. I also know that he has no problem sharing.

But *this girl*.

This girl is different.

I knew it the moment I first laid eyes on her.

She's not a readable person, or she wasn't at first. She feigned confidence, or at least she played off her reserve more than anything. I could tell she was curious when I saw her with Hunter at the club. I felt a pang of jealousy at seeing her on his arm, I'll admit. But there wasn't anything I was going to be able to do about it because *I'm me*. And it didn't help that I had girls hanging all over me at the time.

But I swear, once I get a taste of her, I'll never touch another woman. Ever.

And I can tell that Hunter's eyes are haunted with that same feeling.

She's *ours*.

And we are *hers*.

But one thought invades my mind almost alarmingly. So before I make her take down her jeans, I decide to ask her a question.

"When you came in here, you were looking for Zayd. Any particular reason?"

"I um..." She crosses her arms over her chest, still bare to us with her back against the wall. And I know that my sudden need to ask a rather stupid question creates an awkward space for the time being.

"I needed to talk to him about the script change for tomorrow. There's been a change of plans and it actually includes the two of you as well." Her tone is shaky, and I can tell she's wracked with so much need. "Why?"

"Because I've seen the way he looks at you. And he *doesn't* like to share." I look over to Hunter who gives me a curt nod. An understanding. She's ours... *for now*.

"I just need to be inside of you at least one time before he stakes his claim on you, Nova." I can tell this statement creates a twister of confusion and curiosity fighting a war inside of her, presenting itself across her beautiful face in a very visible blush. "We can talk business later. Are you ready to take us like a good girl, Nova?"

She chews on her bottom lip nervously. There's no sign of the professional, confident woman that was here the day before. Now, she's a shy, needy mess and it's a stunning look on her.

She nods her head greedily.

"Take your pants off for us, sweetheart," I tell her gently.

Hunter pushes off the wall slightly, I can see his excitement. If Hunter stood a chance against Zayd or I on his own, he'd probably be the best option for her. He'd take care of her and be all chivalrous and shit. I would probably shock the hell out of the world and do the same honestly. But we both know that this might be our only night with her before the viper strikes.

Zayden Stone doesn't fuck around, he doesn't do one-night stands, he doesn't play games. He simply looks. And when he laid eyes on Nova, his look was his claim.

And even knowing this information, it's not going to stop me from enjoying the fuck out of worshiping this woman while I can.

Nova has her jeans off, she even pulled her panties down too. *Eager girl.*

The rise and fall of her chest is heavy as she tries desperately to catch her breath.

But we're just getting started.

Hunter saunters over to us, tearing off his shirt in the process. She gasps and I love the way my sweetheart squirms.

I lean down to my mess of a girl and whisper into her ear, "We'll ease you into it baby, but by the time we're done with you, you'll be begging to take both of us at the same time." I push her hair behind her shoulder before trailing my finger down the path of goosebumps covering her skin. I reach the hardened peaks of her breast and pinch the bud between my fingers.

"Mm," she whines.

Hunter slides his hands down her sides and over the curves of her hips and he follows the movement down while positioning himself on his knees in front of her, and despite the envy I'm feeling right now, I see the look of rapture wash over Nova's face, and I would do anything she ever asked me to if it meant I got to see her like this again.

Hunter starts his assault on her pussy. I can see his tongue dart out and swipe between her folds and my sweetheart moans and thrusts.

I'm standing right next to her side, facing her. I can see her face contort with so much enjoyment that it almost reads as pain.

"Touch me, Nova," I whisper darkly into her ear.

She reaches out and grabs at my dick, still tucked behind my shorts but she grips my length anyways and looks at me as she's getting her pussy eaten out.

Fuck, she's beautiful.

"Let me . . . oh shit . . . I want to feel you bare," she says between lusty moans. I smirk at her, so proud that she's asking for what she wants. So I remove my gym shorts and let my dick spring free.

She looks down and she pulls her bottom lip in between her teeth. She wraps her pretty hand around my girth, and gasps. I do too, feeling the softness of her hands sends electricity to my balls and I swear she could just hold me just like this and I'd come.

Hunter finally decides to insert his fingers into her entrance. I know because I can hear how wet she is when he does. That and her attention turns to him on his knees.

"Does he fill you good enough, sweetheart?" I ask, leaning in to kiss her neck.

While Hunter praises her on his knees, and she grips my cock tightly, starting to thrust to the beat of Hunter's fingers, I decide to slide my hand down her front and help her over the edge.

I pinch her bundle of nerves between my fingers before circling it relentlessly. She pulls her other hand up over her mouth and writhes as we make her feel so fucking good.

My mind takes over and I decide I want to make this extra intense for her, so I take my other hand and seize the moment she arches off the wall, sliding my hand between the cement and her ass only to slip my fingers between her ass cheeks finding that tight circle of muscle. I press my finger gently past the entrance creating a little pressure and her eyes roll back as her whole body starts to shake.

I still play with her clit with my other hand and her own grip on my dick becomes so lazy because of how much she's taking from us. Hunter's groans vibrate through to both of us, and I can tell she's so fucking close to losing herself in the depths of her pleasure.

She's everything a man could dream of. Her body is so fucking curvy and sexy. I can see stretch marks guarding her upper thighs and around her belly and I swear to all that is fucking holy that I've never seen anything more beautiful than her. Her honey-colored hair is a matted and sweaty mess against her forehead and back. Her breasts bounce heavily with every thrust Hunter gives her. The sounds she makes as I play with her from both sides.

And the look in her eyes as she tells me she's finally going to come.

"Take it, sweetheart. You said you wanted to come now fucking take it." I speed up my pace on her clit and my other finger presses a little further. And before I know it, she's a mess of tears and cries of gratification and body shakes and curse words.

She's a fucking sin.

And I don't know how I'm going to let her go.

Eleven

Nova

My body is on fire. Both of these men worked together to make me come and the shock of how dangerously good it felt is still coursing through me in violent waves.

But does this make me a slut? A whore? I just started working here not more than twenty-four hours ago and I've already let two of the star wrestlers unravel me in ways I never imagined.

It feels forbidden and wrong. What if they think differently of me? What if they don't respect me because of this?

But when I look back at Hunter and Krew, both men standing just a few feet back to let me catch my breath, I don't see judgment and I don't see shame.

I see them looking at me the same way they do after they've won a match. Though I start to feel guilty for allowing so much fulfillment and pleasure from what just happened that it causes the defense mechanism of over thinking to take over.

But sex doesn't have to be some kind of sentimental thought-provoking experience. Some people are built with needs and fantasies. And it's okay to just enjoy those, regardless of what anyone might think. Besides, neither one of these men made me feel anything less than cherished. They made my body and soul feel safe. Giving yourself over to those needs and fantasies is a risk of displeasure and disappointment but they've given me the opposite and more.

That's the feeling that skates its way to the forefront and it's what I latch onto because it's what makes me feel the most alive.

Awakened.

I'm not a slut or maybe I am and I just don't care, but they're not looking at me like I am. There's nothing wrong with feeding your sexual desires, even if you didn't know you had them in you.

"You look so pretty when your pussy sings for us, little one." Hunter's soft tone is laced with adoration, complimenting me when I didn't think I could be complimented.

Growing up was hard. Especially being made fun of for who my dad was and the way I looked. And now, all of that negativity is being wiped away completely.

Being told I'm beautiful and pretty and seeing how badly I turn on these men ignites the fire for more inside of me. Though I never sought out their approval, having given it to myself because I'm proud of who I am. But I'd be lying if I said that having their attention and approval doesn't give me motivation and power.

And I want more from them.

My men.

Hunter wipes his mouth with the back of his hand while Krew removes his shorts entirely. My heart rate picks up again, nervous for what to expect next—not really knowing there will be a next.

His dick bobs as he walks over to me, and I can feel my stomach tighten with excitement. "What do you want now, sweetheart?" he asks me. Though I don't think he really needs to ask because I'd seriously let them do whatever they wanted to me right now.

"I want you…" I look at Krew, holding an orgasm-induced stare on him before sweeping my lust-filled eyes over to Hunter, who is still fully clothed. "Both."

His look turns from satisfaction to hunger as he yanks me into him and lifts me up, my legs naturally wrapping around his torso. I'm starting to love the feeling of being in his arms like this. How he can so easily lift me up and hold me like I'm his to cherish and hold.

The corded muscles in his arms and chest bulge as he grips me and presses us together tightly.

He squeezes me into the wall again and I can feel the head of his cock whispering against my pussy. He kisses me, his lips demanding to dance with mine and I let him take my mouth roughly. Just as our tongues find each other, he pushes me down onto his dick, his groan is guttural and low, and I gasp from how full he makes me.

There's pain, but only for a second. He's big, I can feel his length stretch me. I close my eyes as I try to adjust, pressing my hands down on his shoulders for purchase. He removes my back from the cold wall which makes me tighten my grip around his torso, still keeping my eyes closed as he thrusts slowly at first.

"You feel so good, Nova. You ready for one more?" Just as his last word escapes his mouth in a raspy breath, I feel body heat scoot in behind me so I open my eyes and look over my shoulder to see Hunter fitting himself beautifully against the wall, putting me dead in the middle of the both of them. My breath hitches as I feel his finger slide down my spine and between the valley of my ass where he presses his thumb into the tight hole there.

"It's going to hurt, Nova. But we know you can take us. Just focus on what feels good, okay?" Hunter's whispers bring me some relief as Krew continues to thrust slowly.

I know this is what I asked for but I can't help but feel the panic rise up from my stomach and into my throat, ready to push its way out in the form of a verbal red light. But I don't have time to make up my mind before I feel the tip of Hunter's dick push past the tightness slowly.

"Ow," I cry, leaning into Krew's neck.

Krew still holds me seamlessly to his chest while is dick is in my pussy. He stops his thrusting so that I can adjust to Hunter's size.

Hunter is gripping my hip with one hand as the other hangs on to my shoulder.

"Shh, it's okay baby. Relax and take it. You can do it." I listen to Krew's comfort as I try to relax to the feeling of having both holes so incredibly filled.

"God, it's tight, Nova. Just breathe so I can fit." Hunter removes his hand from my shoulder and runs it up and down my back in the most soothing way. Like he's telling me I can do this, like he cares about how it's going to feel for me. He's trying to calm me down and it's fucking working.

I close my eyes and relax, letting the tension leave my body when I exhale slowly and allow Hunter to push himself further.

"Wait!" I say leaning back and looking at Krew. "I'm not on birth control, and you're..." I look down between us. I feel Hunter slowly pushing forward and I feel the pressure start to rise.

"I can pull out if you want me to, Nova. Paint you with my seed instead. But imagine how fucking sexy you'd look pregnant with my child while we fuck you like this." Krew's words give me so many butterflies for reasons I can't explain. My cheeks hurt from how fevered they become and that's when I feel Hunter give one last thrust, his dick deep in my asshole.

I twitch from the invasion, a tear escaping my eye. It hurts and I want to tell him to stop, then Krew starts thrusting again and all I can feel is the pressure from both of them pushing into me and vibrating to my clit, creating a masterpiece of pain and pleasure.

"I-I don't want to get pregnant," I admit. But I don't tell them to stop because I realize that I might enjoy the thrill. Will he be able to pull out fast enough? I can tell that that's the same look in his eyes. Like it's a game he wants to play.

"Fuck, Krew. She's so tight back here. God if only she can see how beautifully she takes both of us."

I decide to stop talking and adjust to the feeling of both of these men fucking me. It's painful but I keep myself steady with my palms over Krew's shoulders while both men continue their bruising grips into my skin, fighting for purchase as they both thrust.

It hurts having Hunter back there, but I start to feel dizzy with so much pleasure when I feel his hand reach around my stomach and skate slowly down to my pussy. He presses his middle finger to my clit and they both pound into me in unison.

"Holy shit," I cry. Being held up by both men and being treated like a slut feels so fucking good right now.

"God, baby," Krew groans behind gritted teeth before he leans down and sucks my nipple into his mouth.

"Say that thing again, little one. What did you call me the other night?" Hunter mentions and I nearly freeze, wondering if Krew knew about that or not. Also feeling guilt for how he might feel if he didn't know. But he shows no hesitation as he looks me in the eye and waits for me to respond.

And I know exactly what Hunter is asking for.

"Daddy," I whisper in a lusty groan, speaking to Hunter but looking at Krew.

"I can't hear you," Hunter says as he speeds his thrusts.

I keep my eye contact lined with Krew's as my face heats, and he stares into me with a visceral need of his own.

"He didn't hear you, sweetheart. Say it again," Krew demands me as he too quickens his pace.

"Fuck, daddy." I feel the knot of need start to unravel in my core and damn near ready to burst.

"That's right, baby. I'm your fucking daddy. The only one you need," Hunter grounds out in violent breaths.

"We'll treat you so fucking good, Nova. Make this pussy feel so fucking full," Krew adds and their praise and attention adds to my deadly desire of just wanting to be appreciate, sending me into a spiral of blurred vision and intense ecstasy.

"I'm gonna come," I whimper behind my moans and string of curse words.

"Look at the mirror, little one. Watch yourself come on our cocks. See how pretty you are while you sing for us." Hunter speeds up his assault on my clit while I do what he asks, finding the mirror that lines the wall on the other side of the room.

I focus my eyes on the mirror. It's not super close but I can see the tangled mess of sweat and sex that we are.

That's when I feel it. The pull of heat and hunger.

Dark.

Black.

Irises.

Zayd.

He's watching me as I get pulverized by two of his colleagues. I don't see much else of him as he's tucked away in the shadows. The door is open a sliver and while I can't see all of him, he can see all of me.

I don't know why he stands there or when he got here. Part of me wants him to enter the room and join me. *Join us.*

I hold eye contact with Zayd while Hunter and Krew bring me to the edge. A cliff so deep that it feels almost painful falling off it but I throw myself over anyways and my face pinches and contorts, rendering me painfully aroused as I feel the waves crash over me.

"Such a good girl taking us like this, Nova." Hunter praises me while I ride out my orgasm. Both of them are doing their part to provide me with the most pleasure I can extract from them all while I look into my shadow's eyes.

It's intense and I feel the last wave crash its course and I close my eyes for a second to gain composure. But when I open them again, he's gone.

Hunter's groans come first as I feel his dick throb inside me, his release pummeling through him the way it did me.

Then Krew looks at me as he grips the base of his cock with one hand and I can tell he's on the cusp as well. "Want me to pull out, sweetheart? Or do you want me to pump you so full so you can feel how good the risk of carrying my child might feel?" He almost can't get out the words, he's so turned on and he's trying his hardest to prevent his own fall over the edge.

I look between his deep brown eyes and his cock and I don't have it in me to speak, I still can't fucking breathe from the orgasm that just shredded through me, legs still shaking as they hold me between them.

I see Krew's abs contract and his dick pulses against my walls and I feel the nerves wrack my body wondering what he's going to do. Then right as a deep groan rips through his throat, he pulls himself out and paints the inside of my thighs with his cum. Rope after silky rope, his release coating my skin.

Hunter pulls himself out gently and I feel the immediate pain take over, feeling sore as Krew lowers me back down to my feet.

"You did so good," Krew coos as he brushes my hair behind my ear in a delicate caress. He leans down and presses a soft kiss to my lips while Hunter does the same to the back of my shoulders.

Full. Wanted. Treasured.

That's how these two made me feel just now. That's how I've wanted to feel my whole life, and no one has been able to give that to me.

When I walk away from today, I might feel regret or shame later, but I refuse to let myself believe that I didn't deserve this.

After the boys help me get my clothes gathered—Krew giving me one of his clean shirts from his bag to replace my torn-to-piece blouse—I look at the clock on the wall and see that it's been an hour since I first walked into this room.

An hour.

Did anyone notice or question my absence?

What was I thinking? Is this the kind of person I've become?

"We can't do this again," I say out loud, letting my inner dialogue scratch its way to the surface without so much as a calm thought to subtle the guilt building inside of me.

It's not directed at one or the other, but to both. And I'm rendered shocked when Hunter's laugh reverberates through the silence.

"Why are you laughing?" I ask.

"He's laughing because you're funny, sweetheart. And crazy, if we're being honest," Krew answers as he gets his shoes on.

"I'm being serious. I could lose my job if anyone finds out what went on in here and I honestly can't afford to make this mistake again." I stand up after getting my own shoes on and look into the mirror to see that my hair is completely wrecked. I look around for my phone but don't see it anywhere.

"You *look* serious, but that's the problem. You see…" Hunter approaches me and I retreat, walking backwards until I'm stopped by a dumbbell placed on the floor. "Whether it's with us, or with *him*, you've been claimed, little one. And I'm sorry to break it to you, but as long as you're here, you're ours." He swipes his hand through his blonde waves.

"Looks like the whole good-guy act from yesterday has vanished. And you said you *weren't* a player." I roll my eyes at Hunter, he stops short from his path to me and I use this moment to search the surrounding area for my phone.

"There are no games being played here, Nova. We gave you what you wanted and now you have to give us what we want," Krew chimes in while he packs up his gym bag.

"And what might that be, Mr. Rivers?" I cross my arms at my chest, giving both of them a controlling glare hoping that whatever antics they're playing at will dissipate.

"And she's back to the formalities." Hunter rolls his eyes.

"You," Krew states. Plain and clear.

And I'd be lying if I said that didn't make my pussy throb . . . again. Because I want to keep this up. I really do. But

I worked hard for this job and I can't lose it on day two because I decided to let my sexual desire drown me in the likes of these two.

"That's the thing, I don't belong to anyone and as much fun as this was, it can't happen again." I cluck my tongue and go back to looking for my phone, now convinced that one of them is holding it hostage as some kind of joke.

"Nova, I don't think you heard us." Hunter rubs at the back of his neck, almost as if he's concerned that I'm not accepting what they're saying.

Krew walks over to me until we're toe to toe. He reaches into the pocket of his gym bag and grabs my phone. *That bastard.* I go to take it from him but he grips it tightly as he holds it between us. He uses his other hand to tip my chin up toward him.

"You're ours. And if I get another moment alone with you, you better hope that you'll be ready for me. Because I'll have you begging so prettily for my cock, it'll make your pussy hurt. And I promise to give it to you just right, sweetheart. Because you fucking deserve it and you know you do." Krew lets go of my phone, backs away, grabs his bag and heads for the door without another word.

"See you around, little one." Hunter attempts to join him, but I stop him by grabbing gently onto his wrist. He turns to face me.

"Do you guys do this to all the women you see? It's like a game of kickball to you. Kicking the girl around to see who can score the goal first?" I spit out, not half as angry as I'm presenting myself, because like I said, I wanted this. But I also want them to explain themselves.

"Earlier, when you were coming on my tongue or on Krew's cock with both of us so deep inside you, did it feel like you were being kicked around? Or did it feel like teamwork? Because I'm pretty sure it looked like you were being appreciated by your teammates, baby. And I think that makes you the winner." Hunter leans in and presses a kiss to my cheek before following Krew out the door.

I'm frozen for a moment, thinking about what he'd just said and he's right. I do feel like a winner as cliché as that sounds.

My phone buzzes in my hand and I look down to see I've got two unread texts. The first one from nearly thirty minutes ago reads:

> That's strike 2.

The text that just came through...

> 3.

What the fuck? It's from the same number as yesterday and I try to think of who this could be from.

I hit the call button and the phone goes straight to a generic voicemail. Typical.

It can't be Hunter or Krew can it? Maybe it's just another game they're playing next to the one they claim to *not* be playing.

Then my mind crosses to earlier... Zayden.

How he keeps watching me.

How he knows where to find me and seemingly hunts me down for no fucking reason. But why in the world would he be texting me this cryptic bullshit?

And why does the thrill of this unknown turn me on?

Twelve

Nova

It's been one hell of a couple of days but tonight is the night. Friday Night Beatdown. I hang out with the stage folk and some commentators out near the stage while the wrestlers are currently staged in dress rooms.

We're getting ready to bring my idea to life, *live* on national television.

I look around and imagine that my family would be proud. At least my mom would be. But my father, that's a truthfully, predictable easy no.

Maybe he'd find out what I did and call me an even bigger disappointment then he made me feel. Maybe his only daughter is actually disgracing the family name by being here.

But now's not the time for those intrusive thoughts. I bite back the sting of tears threatening to break the damn and do what I do best.

Pretend.

Pretend that my father would actually approve of who I grew up to be and acknowledge my accomplishments.

We move around the stage and pinpoint the best camera angles as I go over the script with everyone one more time.

Before I know it, fans start to fill the audience seating, the stadium surrounding us starts to echo with laughter and roars as people of all ages grab their seats with their favorite wrestlers' merch or their big, colorful signs.

My eyes widen in appreciation, remembering what it was like to be one of them. Fuck my dad, because if he's not proud of me, I'm fucking proud of me.

Part of me wonders if I followed this career path because it was some kind of fucked up way for me to seek his approval, even though he's not alive for me to justify that. But while that may still have some truth to it, it's this moment right now that I know I did this for me.

"Alright everyone. The show starts soon. Time to head backstage." Shawn waves everyone out of the stage area and we all march up the ramp toward the back arena.

Before I exit, I turn around one more time to soak in the euphoric feeling that is the sport of wrestling and I smile, knowing that the little girl in me is screaming.

That's when I see a small child, she looks to be about seven or eight. She reminds me of me a little bit. Her pigtails are curled and she's wearing a bright pink princess dress.

"It's beautiful. Isn't it, little one?" I look over to see that Hunter and Krew are both standing at my side, tucked behind the curtains but still able to be seen by onlookers.

"What are you two doing out here? You should be in the dress rooms." I suddenly feel my excitement melt into danger. But it's a danger laced with ashes of lust, burning delicately across my skin and leaving me hot yet again.

"We have time for some autographs." They both dip past me, neither attempting to avoid brushing my skin with their own, smirks on both of their devilishly smug faces.

"Wait." I stop them and look back out to the little girl I noticed moments ago. "The one with the princess dress, start with her please." I nod to the girl who sits with her mom. They both look her way before giving me their approval.

"Anything for you, sweetheart." Krew leans in and presses a gentle kiss to my lips and I fight the way it makes me feel.

Emotional?

I told them we couldn't do what we did again. And I meant it. Or at least I pretended to. But something secretive and coveted caresses my insides as I watch them walk away until they approach the little girl.

I watch a few moments longer to see her face light up and her mom's reaction is just as awe worthy. I smile to myself before dipping back behind the curtains and start to walk down the hall to meet up with the others.

But a force so intense stops me in my tracks.

And I know that he's here.

"What do you want, Mr. Stone?"

I turn around and catch sight of the shadow lingering down the hall. I can feel him staring at me, it's like cold, steel bullets piercing through my skin.

"I warned you, Nova. And I will stay true to my promise." A deep voice rumbles through the hallways and proves just how weak my body is when I feel the shockwave of his rough timber vibrate in my center as he says my name.

I can't make out anything other than his shadow. The lights in the hallways he's standing in are off, whereas I'm standing in nothing but pure bright light.

"So you're the mysterious texter." I find the courage to say, even though I assumed as much.

"I will come for you, little star. On the count of three." And before I have time to process what the fuck any of what he just said meant, the shadow is gone and I'm once again weak to my unannounced and certainly indescribable arousal.

But I won't let some controlling psycho ruin this night. This is *my* night.

It's two hours into the show. I've watched most of it from backstage but the main event is about to start and I shamelessly begged Darnel to let me out into the arena. Normally, backstage crew members don't get front row seats but he accepted my pleas and got me as close as he could.

To my surprise I'm standing right next to the princess, literally front row to the ring, and she gives me a smile before the lights change and the music starts indicating the start of the main event.

A bassy remix of *Reverse* by Sage The Gemini takes over the stadium speakers and picks up in a roar as the lights go black save for the blood red strobes that set off in a scattered pattern across the crowd. Two men walk out from behind the curtain and stand at the top of the center stage.

"Ladies and gentlemen. Now introducing, for the main event title match, the undisputed tag-team champions, KREWWWW RIIIIVERRRSSS AND HUUNTERRR DODGGGEEE." Pyrotechnics go off around them as the announcer's voice vibrates through the crowd. The audience goes crazy. Mostly in a spine tingling reaction of cheers and shouts. I swear I even hear a chick beg Krew to be her baby daddy. *If only she knew.*

I look behind me to see signs thrown up in the air and kids sit on their dad's shoulders while their mom's cheer unashamedly. Everyone eats up their entrance as they strut halfway down, carrying their championship belts while sporting their tight-pant ensembles before taking off in a full run and sliding into the ring under the first rope.

My heart threatens to break out of its confines from how hard it's pounding in my chest. The adrenaline rush I feel as I watch these men interact with the crowd as it breaks into fits of applause, the lights still flashing around us as their music dies down.

Even the little girl is wide-eyed and in awe.

Before the next team is announced, Krew makes quick work of showing off as he rips his shirt off his body, he looks at me and only me as he does it and I have to bow my head and hide my blush as my stomach fills with butterflies.

A funky beat starts up and red, white and blue lights take over the headlights.

"Introducing their opponents. And competing for the tag-team championship title. JUUUUUSSTIIIIIIN RIIICK-YYYY AND LUUUKAAAAA VAAAAANCE. THE U. K. O. BROOOTTHEEERRSSSS." The announcer's voice, once again, rumbles over the crowd before she turns to leave the ring.

Krew uses his foot to hold down the bottom rope for her while Hunter lifts the middle allowing her to bend down gracefully and safely exits down the steps.

The ref enters the center of the ring while one member of each team exits and stands on the outskirts. Hunter stands in the center with his opponent, Luka. They look completely in their element.

The bell rings signaling the start of the match and everyone cheers in excitement.

The match goes on for about fifteen minutes. They've tagged out at least two times each at this point, But now, it's Hunter and Justin.

Justin has Hunter in a headlock. To the little girl next to me, it looks life-threatening. To me, I can tell it wouldn't be all that hard to escape. But I won't fill her in on my secret. Instead, I cheer with her. Screaming for Hunter to break free. I'm glad she's cheering for the same team I am.

I see Krew reach his hand over the ring rope, offering a chance for Hunter to tag him in. But Justin pulls Hunter further into the center of the ring and away from his chance to get free. Justin keeps hold of his headlock for about thirty more seconds before Hunter lifts his weight, pushing his shoulders into his opponent's chest and lifts his feet off the ground. Everyone gets louder as Hunter has Justin's arms still wrapped around his neck but he's regained leverage. He lets out one big grunt and pushes his entire weight, throwing Justin over his shoulder, releasing his hold, and landing him back first into the mat.

That's my boy.

He trots over to Krew and tags him in. Krew jumps the ropes as Hunter exits and the crowd explodes again.

Krew walks over to the guy laying on the floor and lifts him up by his arms and drags him to one of the turnbuckles, positioning him so that he's sitting up against the corner.

Krew runs to the diagonal corner, bouncing off the turnbuckle before he runs toward Justin and shoulders him in the chest.

That was real.

And it looked painful.

Like I said, most of it is scripted but some of the stunts they pull are real.

Justin lies there, seemingly helpless as Krew repeats the move, running from corner to corner. But this time, Justin rolls his body over just as Krew reaches the turnbuckles and ends up ramming into the hardness of the corner instead.

He winces and holds his shoulder, and I know that has to hurt whether he can take it or not. The crowd starts to boo as Justin tags his other member and Luka immediately starts whaling on Krew.

Of course, you can hear the slaps of skin on skin as Luka swings his hand against Krew's chest but it's all a ploy, a sound effect to feign real action. But it's exciting, nonetheless. Krew seems to slump under his attack and his opponent mimics Krew's last move. But before he can make it off the opposing turnbuckle, Hunter reaches out and twists Luka's arm so that he's facing Hunter and Hunter swings his fist at Luka's face. This garner's an argument from the ref as the crowd cheers in approval.

Hunter is now fighting with the ref as Luka stumbles to the center of the mat from Hunter's blow and this gives Krew a chance at a pin. He pushes Luka down the rest of the way so he's flat on his back and he throws his arms over his chest.

The ref is still fake arguing with Hunter about his cheating agenda and the crowd counts down.

"ONE. TWO. THREE." But the countdown doesn't matter if the ref didn't catch it. Right before the ref finally turns around, Justin reaches under the ropes and yanks Luka by his feet, sliding him out from under Krew's body and out of the ring.

The crowd boos as the cowards stay standing on the outskirts of the ring just at the base of the ramp while Krew and Hunter egg them on to get back in the ring.

The UKO Brothers have their backs to the stage as they catch their breath. If the ref had been paying attention, Krew would have won that. But that's now how the script goes. I did write most of their story, so I anticipate the next move.

That's when the lights turn off right on cue, and the arena goes black. The crowd knows what this means. Screams of excitement erupt as flashlights from phones light up the arena.

A slow beat starts. The crowd quiets down as they wait for the beat drop of a deep and bassy rendition of *Mount Everest* to implode which also signals the effect of creepy, white lights flashing in three seconds spurts.

The small amount of light allows us to see the UKO Brothers feign fear as they look around frantically for who's about to come out.

The crowd chants, in unison, the words to his intro song.

"*CUZ I'M TOP OF THE WORLD!*"

Then suddenly fireworks explode from their prospective stances in spurts right as the beat drops hard and the sexy devil himself emerges from the center stage. The lights start to dim back on, and his music starts to die down just as he makes a break for it down the ramp. The UKO Brothers have no time to escape before Zayd spears both of them, head bowed to guide him into the space between them and his arms strike at their chests at the same time as he drives through them, knocking them flat on their asses.

He stands up straight while flipping his dark, wet, curls over his head and he roars into the sky. His fists stretched out on either side of him as his chest vibrates from the roar that rips from his throat.

The crowd cheers him on in the chaotic fashion of a passionate fandom.

I feel it.

Everywhere.

And he gives me a thigh-clenching, heated glance before he jumps into the ring and stands in the middle of Hunter and Krew.

Looking at them in their zone—all three of them together in the middle of the glorious ring herself—causes so many different feelings to circulate throughout me. Listening to the crowd chant all of their names as they witness an unexpected chain of events and it makes me proud.

It only takes a few more seconds for the UKO Brothers to almost be disqualified by count out but just as the ref shouts ten, the boys jump into the ring and *my* boys jump to action.

Zayden grabs Justin by the wrist and tosses him over his shoulder. At the same time, Luka gets pushed back and forth between Krew and Hunter before one of them clotheslines him. Zayden finally tosses Justin on his back before turning and jumping up just to drive down into him with his elbow.

Both of the UKO Brothers are now pinned. Luka is under Krew and Hunter, and Justin under Zayd as the ref and the crowd start the countdown.

"ONE. TWO. THREE!"

Music explodes in tandem with the roars of approval from the crowd. Santana Ingles, the announcer, stands up from her chair and starts the winning announcements.

"Ladiiiiiesss and gentlemennnnn. Your winnnerrrrsss. And still the UNDISPUTED tag-team champions, KREWWWW RIIIIVERRRSSS AND HUUNTERRR DODGGGEEE. Accompanied by, and still your UWE world heavyweight champion, ZAYYYDENNNN STOOOONNNNE!" The little girl next to me claps gleefully while her mama cheers with her.

The rest of the crowd shouts and chants as confetti floats from the ceiling and pyrotechnics erupt from all around the stadium.

The boys all hold up their belts as they scan the crowd and roar their alpha-male roars.

But my heart stops when Zayden turns to look at me, dead in the eyes for what feels like a solid minute. And right before he jumps out of the ring he mouths something to me.

"*RUN*." Panic rises as he lands on the ground and stalks toward me. Run? *What the hell does he want me to run from?*

What a minute . . . he wants me to run from *him*.

I decide to do myself a favor and listen to him, taking off in a hurry through the crowd and back toward the stage.

I jog up the stairs, so as not to trip, and hide behind the curtains.

But I don't believe he's chasing me, not in a stadium full of people.

So I turn to peek out from behind the curtain and I see that he's signing the princess's UWE poster.

My heart fucking melts. But just as quickly, I recognize danger when he looks straight at me and walks past everyone else, heading my way.

Almost as if he's stalking his prey.

"Oh fuck," I whisper to myself before bolting into the back halls.

WRESTLING

LITTLE STAR

little one

wrestling

Thirteen
Nova

Adrenaline eats at my stomach and my heart beats heavily against my chest like a drum. I'm actually running, well jogging now because I'm out of breath. And I don't know how far back he is or where I'm supposed to run to. I don't know very many rooms back here and honestly, I don't even know why he's chasing me to begin with.

I turn a corner after looking back to see if I spot him down the hallway, but the coast is clear. I'm panting when I reach a woman's bathroom and decide that this has to be the safest place for me right now.

I give myself a mental pat on the back for wearing sensible shoes today, paired with black, ripped skinny jeans and a loosely tied Poison shirt.

I close the door to the bathroom and lock it, before sliding down to the floor and waiting.

I wonder if anyone will miss me, not knowing how long I have to keep this up for. My phone reads nearly nine thirty at night right now.

My sporadic breathing has time to settle while I appreciate the course of the show tonight. In my head, it went perfect, but being perfect in real life is entirely different and I'd say the show was a killer success.

I lean into the door to listen for steps or voices, but nothing ever comes.

Thirty minutes pass by, I still hear absolutely nothing.

I'm such an idiot. I've accused Hunter and Krew of playing games but the one really screwing around is Zayden.

I get up from the floor and unlock the door gently. Knowing my luck, he'd be standing right there the whole time and I'd not know it.

But there's no one there when I push the door open and step out into the now darkened hall.

I'm pretty sure everyone went home. I've never really known what happens to the crew and cast when big shows like this end, but I just need to find my way out of here.

I turn on my phone's flashlight—I've never really been one to be afraid of the dark, but it's still creepy as fuck being back here all by myself—and I walk through the halls trying to retrace my steps and go back to where I started.

It doesn't take me long to recognize the curtains leading to the arena so I shimmy my way out and realize that I was right, everyone is long gone by now.

Even the cleaning crew have finished their jobs.

I decide to take this moment to walk back out to the stage, slowly padding down the ramp and making my way toward the center of entertainment.

But it's empty and cold and lifeless as the ring is presented naked to me, free from the fight and the men who act it out, and the seats are filled with silence.

It's a beautiful thing to be a witness to the chaos that is controlled here only to see that chaos be stripped down to a calm and quiet scene.

I reach the steps to the arena and decide to climb on, dipping between two ropes, imagining the crowd screaming and cheering.

I love thinking about what it would be like to have a fanbase, even though wrestling has never been in my foreseeable future as a competitor. Or to have an audience or a team of my own.

The idea warms me as I look around in the darkness of the empty stadium.

"Nova."

A strong, rough, growly voice breaks through the silence and nearly brings me to fucking knees. Either because it scars me or because it sounds too much like a seductive trap.

I turn quickly to find the source and my eyes stop at the end of the ramp, not more than ten feet from the ring, to see a shadow lurking.

Zayd.

"I don't have time for your stupid games, Mr. Stone. I was just about to leave so you can get lost now." I try my best to feign control but I know he can hear the shiver in my voice.

I'm also no stranger to the knot of electricity unraveling in my core, sprouting out to every nerve ending in my body.

But I should be frustrated, this man made me run and hide for nothing other than a good laugh, I'm assuming.

"You shouldn't talk to me like that," he demands and it's almost laughable.

"Your god complex is showing, Zayd. You might want to go tend to that," I snark and before I get a chance to express regret, Zayden is pulling himself up to the ring by the ropes and jumps into the center. I stumble back until my back is up against a corner of turnbuckles.

Zayd rushes in, caging me in the corner as he mentally deprives my lungs of air.

"I'm no god, little star. I am your Hell and I will ruin you." His words bite at my skin before settling over me in a warm and inviting promise.

Lord.

What could I have possibly done to him to make him feel like he has to ruin me? I feel so helplessly trapped under him like this, he towers over me and his dark features add so much sex appeal to this already confusing position I'm in.

He smells like amber and oak moss. It's un-fucking-real what the effect of his scent is doing to my brain. It's like a paralytic, rendering me frozen while nearly panting in desire.

"That's real noble of you, Mr. Stone but I-" his black eyes burn through my skin as I try to formulate a tangible sentence. But I can't. Because the only thing I can feel or hear is the invading pulse of my heated heart and the throb between my legs.

"I've been watching you parade this pretty pussy around for everyone to grab ahold of." His whisper is dark and deep between us, and I should be insulted by his accusation. But I know he's not really wrong. But what matter does it have to him?

He reaches out and drags a rough finger along my cheek, causing my breath to hitch.

"You're mine." He returns his hands to hold himself up by gripping the top line of ropes on either side of my head. I'm crushed against the hard leather balls that dig into my back and I can't seem to conjure up a controlled thought.

"Say it, Nova," he growls as he watches me become an absolute puddle to his voice, craving every demand he's willing to give me.

"I'm-" I swallow, trying to resist the urge to give him what he wants but I know I'd just be lying if I denied it.

Tension ignites between us as he licks his lips. I can't deny I loved being with Hunter and Krew, but the way this man simply looks at me is all I'll ever need to die a happy woman.

"I'm yours," I say in uncertainty, but knowing I love the way it sounds.

We've not said more than a few sentences to each other since I started working here, so this integration should seem so out of pocket. But it's desire and fantasy that drives my need to allow this happen.

He removes his hands from one of the ropes and leans down to grip the back of my neck. He's ripping through baby hair at the nape as he squeezes and pushes me forward so that my lips are next to his ear.

"Again," he demands, tone deep and guttural.

"I'm yours, Zayd," I breathe on a lusty pant.

The look of approval swirls through Zayden's devilish eyes when he leans down and presses his lips to my ear.

"I'm so fucking proud of you." His whisper is so viscerally deep and broken but it doesn't make it any less meaningful. "I know what you did tonight and I am so fucking proud." His words of praise light my skin on fire, my eyes reading his in the darkened space between us.

Appreciation builds heavily in my bones as I drown myself in the way it feels to be locked in this position with the most powerful man in the world, telling me he's proud of me,

He leans back and we both stare at each other, me with confusion and lust and him with hunger and pride.

It's a damning sight, the light and the dark. And it's in this moment that I realize that Krew was right.

This is his *claim*.

He wants me and I think I want him. I've always wanted him. Way before I entered the ring.

I liked being shared, but something about his claim on me renders me completely loyal to the way it feels when he looks at me. Only me.

"What did you mean by that . . . by that first text you sent me?" I decide to ask, only because I need to put some kind of buffer between us so that my lungs can play catch up.

"I meant exactly what I said, Nova." The hunger that laces his tone strikes me like a lightning bolt zipping through my spine.

It's the source of heat that sits between my thighs and makes my insides twist in desire.

"I have a job to do here, Mr. Stone. I don't have time to be playing these childish games." It's the first time I feel confident while speaking to him. My words don't come out broken or confused.

I undo the tension I've held in my shoulders by letting myself relax against the turnbuckles that still dig into my back. I suck in a few much needed breaths when Zayden sits back on his knees, giving us about a foot or two between us.

Just when I thought I might finally get a chance to talk him out of whatever this is, he grips me by my ankles and slides me down roughly so that my back is flat on the mat.

He leans over me, doing no justice to the ache in my core and not caring how rough he's being.

"Zayden, wha-what are you doing?"

He brings his mouth down to my ear and I can hear him lick his lips before he growls darkly, "Sometimes, your only job is to get pinned, little star. Now, hold still and don't you dare think about running. I don't like chasing my meal."

Zayden feverishly pops the button of my jeans and yanks them down my legs. The action is so fast I can't even fight my way out of the invasion, and I don't want to. I want this, Him. More than I want anything else in this world.

The second the cold air hits the wetness that soaks into my panties, my fit of panic melts into a puddle. And my craving for this man heightens intensely.

After he's got my shoes and jeans off, he tosses everything over the ropes of the ring. His fingers pull at the seem of my underwear stretching them out so that he has better access to my pussy and after he's pulled the fabric so tightly that it nearly cuts into my skin, he pushes my legs up so that my knees are at my chest and he leans in, not taking a second longer to taste just how wet I am for him.

His tongue swipes between my folds and I do everything not to squirm and scream.

The position he's forced me in and the pleasure he's drawing from me is worth the fact that anyone can come into this arena and hear my cries of ecstasy echo in the distance.

"Fuck," I cry when he laps at my clit. His guttural groans vibrate through me and everything that's holding me together is damn near about to explode.

My back arches off the mat when he pushes his fingers into my entrance and I can hear how fucking wet I am.

He removes his mouth to watch him finger me.

"Your pussy was hungry, baby. Look how badly you needed me." Zayden is wearing tight black pants, a plain black t shirt and his hair is now tied up in his infamous topknot. I feel so dirty when I remember where I'm at and who I'm with. But not dirty in a shameful way. Dirty as in this scene is too fucking sexy for me to fathom and I feel guilty because I like it.

He pumps his fingers in a few more times and I'm already so fucking close to coming undone.

I attempt to touch myself, to find my clit so that I can get rid of this ache. But as soon as I make contact, Zayden smacks my hand which simultaneously vibrates through to my pussy. And even though I'm annoyed that he just smacked my hand like a child, I don't miss the way the sting of pain compliments nicely to the need that surges through me.

God, I'm so close. I just need him to-

"Oh my god, Zayd," I moan. He curls his fingers to touch that needy spot inside of me and I feel as though the damn is about to break loose.

I buck against his hand, desperate to ride out my release but right as the start of my orgasm starts to shatter, he removes his fingers and just stares at me.

"No, no, no. What the fuck?" I pull myself up. His smirk pisses me off as he watches me freak out.

"You asshole," I shout as I reach over and slap my hands against his chest.

He just stays there, sitting back on his knees. I get up, embarrassed because my underwear is stretched so wide that it doesn't even sit right anymore, and my clothes are God knows where. I have to get out of here. I should. But I don't want to.

I attempt to pull the rope down to duck under to leave, but big strong hands yank me back by the curve of my hips and turn me around so that my chest is flush with his.

"I said I was going to discipline you for letting another man touch you, Nova. I was simply staying true to my word." He tilts my chin up, forcing me to look at his dark, black irises. "Now, how would you like to come on my fingers or my cock, little star?" My anger instantly melts into an intoxicating need. I whimper while pulling my lip between my teeth. Why am I letting him do this to me? Why am I so insanely needy for his touch? His approval.

My heart races in my chest as I think about his question and know that nothing is going to rid of this ache and he's handing me the key to my destruction.

"Your cock," I answer in a breathy moan.

No more than a second later, he pulls his shirt over his head with his tattooed arm and I watch the way his muscles flex, the way his entire begin exudes sex and power and how fucking lucky I feel to be the woman before him.

He works his button free before slipping out of his jeans, only left in his boxers now, and walks back into the corner of the ring.

On instinct, I follow him. I position myself in front of him and he reaches for the hem of my shirt. I let him slide it over my head and my breath hitches when he tosses it aside.

He's being gentle now, not rough and aggressive like before. I don't know what I like more.

He pulls me into his chest by my wrists and reaches behind me to unhook my bra. Once he discards that as well, I step out of my underwear and let him evaluate me. But he's not evaluating or analyzing, he's worshipping. His eyes slowly take in my voluptuous body and I can see the satisfaction paint his face.

"You're so fucking beautiful, Nova." I blush at the compliment that comes from his deep tone. The way it vibrates through me is a talent all on its own.

I step in a little closer and reach for his abs. I trace the lines delicately until I'm touching the tops of his boxers. I look up at him to see if he protests but when he doesn't, I drag down his boxers until he's free of them and my mouth waters at the sight of his dick.

It's thick and long and I can't help but lean down and kiss the head.

"Fuck," he groans before he flips me over so that our position is reversed. Now I'm facing the turnbuckles and he's behind me.

He places his palms on my back and pushes me down bending me over. I reach out to find something to hold, landing on the ropes.

I can feel him just staring at me. He steps in a little closer and I feel the tip of his dick feather against my skin.

"Please," I whisper. Anguish pummels through me as I feel so helplessly needy to his touch.

"Please what?" he asks, his voice harsh and rough, just like the way his hands roam my body.

"I need it hard, Zayden. Please."

It was nice of him to take his time to undress me, but I can't hold it in anymore. The ache is painful.

"I've got you, little star." He grabs me by the curve of my hips and pulls me back slightly. I feel the desire swirling inside me as the tip of his dick presses against my entrance.

"Shit," he grunts. "I'll break you, baby. You sure?"

I can feel how big he is, he'll be the biggest I've ever had and I know he's not lying when he says it'll hurt me. But I told him I wanted it hard. And I meant it.

"Break me," I say and he doesn't waste another second before pounding into me from behind with so much force, I feel like I actually shatter.

"Oh," I cry, feeling dizzy in the throes of pleasure.

He stretches me so wide; I feel every vein and ridge of his cock as I try desperately to take in all of him.

"Fuck you feel so fucking good, Nova. Can you feel how perfectly your pussy takes my cock?" He grips me so tightly; his touch is branding my skin.

I push myself back, wanting him to move in and out. The craving for more takes over and I can't think about anything else.

"How does it feel to know that you are mine, little star?" He thrusts into me some more, giving it to me slow, but hard.

"It feels so good, Zayd," I reply. My eyes start to roll back when he picks up his pace and I nearly drown in intense exhilaration.

"This is what you fucking do to me." He squeezes his fingertips into my skin as he rocks into me with so much force that my toes curl into the mat and my vision starts to blur.

He's going faster and faster, deeper and harder.

"Fuck, Zayden. Oh my god." My moans are loud, I'm sure anyone can hear me, but I don't care. I need this. Want this. Zayden fucks me with so much force and so much attention that I could be in front of a whole crowd and not give a damn.

The sound of skin on skin mixing with the sound of how wet I am echoes through the stadium. I lift my head as best I can and imagine an audience full of people watching me get obliterated by their biggest star. And I feel all too much when I realize that I'm *his* star.

I'm so close to coming already, the waves of my desire crashing through me as his harsh breathing creates the perfect harmony to my moans and the sound of us fucking.

"I'm gonna come, Zayd-Oh fuck." I can't help but to let my shrieks of pleasure escape me. And he's fucking me so God damn good that I don't even need to touch my clit because the vibrations from his thrusts are touching me everywhere.

An overwhelming surge of flooding takes over as I come so fucking hard, crying out his name.

"Fuck! Louder, Nova." I can feel his dick pulse against my walls as I grip him and I know he's about to come with me. The idea that he'll come so deep inside me is what sends me over the edge again, before I even recovered from the fall of the first one.

"Oh my god!" I shout when the waves come crashing down. My spine tingles and my cheeks hurt from the heat. My knees almost give out but he doesn't stop pumping me as deep as he can with his thick cock as he releases inside of me.

"Fuck, Nova," he growls, the roar leaving his chest like an exorcism as he finishes inside me. "Jesus, you're gripping me so tight."

Both of us end on labored pants, breathing harsh as the pulse of our orgasm still beats lightly at my core.

He removes himself, and I feel out arousal start to drip down my thighs.

"You needed that, didn't you baby?" Zayden turns me around so that we're face to face.

He brushes my hair away from my eyes while I find a way to breathe again. It's consuming the way he makes me feel. I've never felt anything like that. Even with the boys. The boys made me feel safe and valued. But Zayden made me feel powerful and controlled. I can't explain it, but it's not the same thing.

"I needed *you*," I whisper. I place my palms over his chest, feeling bravery take over as I push him slightly.

I needed all of them in their own ways. I needed Hunter to show me appreciation and that it's okay to want certain things.

I needed Krew to teach me how to ask for what I want and to be confident in wanting them.

And I needed Zayd to challenge me and watch me learn these things about myself along the way so that I could be strong enough to hand myself over to him. So that he could be good enough for me.

I know he won't make me choose. But I know there might only be one choice.

I know this journey was made for him and I. And I know this journey has literally just begun, but sometimes it's not about the middle or the end. Sometimes, it's about the start.

I stand on my tiptoes and pull his head down to meet mine in an all-consuming kiss. Our lips mold together as we explore each other with our tongues.

But I pull away for just a second knowing that now is my chance.

"Nova?" he questions, sensing the curiosity that hangs between us.

"Can you turn around for me?" I ask and he does.

I trace my finger down the script on his spine, trying to make out the words.

las estrellas se alinean

"What's it mean?" I need my curiosity to be answered, seeing this tattoo for so long and never knowing what it meant.

He turns around and faces me once more. His hands come out to either side of my face, caressing my cheeks as he leans down to press another kiss to my lips.

"It means, *the stars align*."

A SPOTLIGHT OF SPICE NOVELLA

WHAT'S NEXT IN THE SERIES?

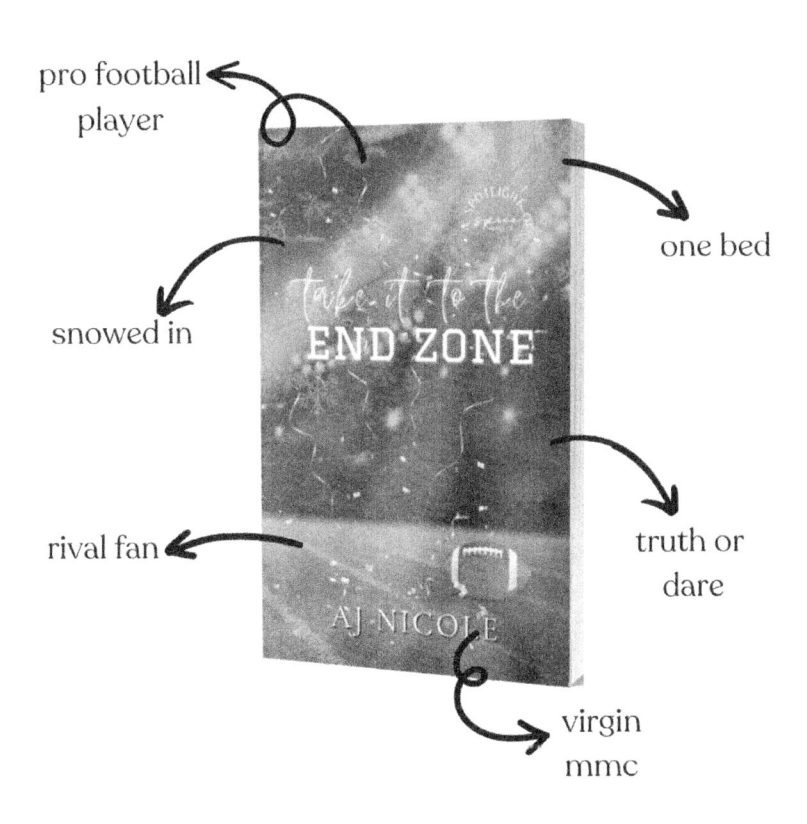

take it to the END ZONE
AJ NICOLE

- pro football player
- snowed in
- rival fan
- one bed
- truth or dare
- virgin mmc

ACKNOWLEDGMENTS

This one is for #booktok. I have a love for pro-wrestling and someone somewhere on that app said, "Turn this into a book," with a video of Roman Reigns and I said, "Bet."

Maryann, thanks for sticking with me and judging but not judging every weird thing you find when you alpha read and edited for me.

For all my readers who hype me up when I seriously question if I'm even doing this right, thanks for always being my biggest cheerleaders and for motivating me to keep going!

Also, for the girlies who have said that my husband somewhat resembles Roman . . . thanks for that lol.

Want to stay updated on all things AJ Nicole? Like when the next book is coming out and where you can find her signing? Visit her website or follow her on social media for more!

Website:
www.booksbyajnicole.com

Social Media:
@booksbyajnicole on both IG & TT

Printed in Great Britain
by Amazon